AF508355

BIONAUT

Ryan R. Moos

RRM PRESS
Topanga, CA

BIONAUT

ISBN 979-8-9951118-1-8 (paperback)

First Edition
Published by RRM Press
Topanga, California
Printed in the United States of America

10 9 8 7 6 5 4 3 2 1

This book is dedicated to all my friends, family, and professional colleagues who told me I have good ideas and to never give up (never surrender).

Chapter 1

The Beast

David "Zabo" Stone woke up on a smooth, cold floor. The room was medium-sized, bare, clinically spartan. He wore nothing but a pair of spandex boyshorts. His body felt strong but drained, as if he'd been asleep too long.

Disoriented, he rubbed his eyes and sat up. The air was cool and sterile—surgical.

On one wall, rows of smooth, metallic hatch doors stretched floor to ceiling. A morgue wall. There must have been a hundred.

Where am I?

He pushed to his feet and steadied himself. A metallic dryness coated his tongue.

A corridor door caught his attention. Stone crossed the room, his footsteps and breathing the only sounds as he shook off a heaviness that felt like a hangover without the pain.

The door slid open, oddly silent, revealing a long corridor. Dark glass lined both sides. Thin white ceiling strips cast a muted glow.

He pressed close to one glass panel. Only blackness outside, with the faintest suggestion of grey desert beyond.

Stone walked about fifty meters until the hallway ended in a pentagon-shaped hub. Four other passages branched away, each identical. He turned left on instinct.

Another hallway. Another morgue-like room. But this one had a second, older-looking door on the far side.

He headed toward it, flanked by the rows of hatch doors. Something on the floor caught his eye—a felt-tip marker, cap missing.

He glanced up at the wall. A small black arrow, hand-drawn and no bigger than his thumb, pointed at the worn door.

Intrigued, he stepped closer. This door didn't open automatically. A recessed white button with a metal ring waited beside it. Stone pressed it. The panel slid aside with a low hiss.

Different.

The hallway beyond was shorter and more industrial. Riveted seams. Exposed hardware. A low hum of power. At the far end, an airlock door blocked the way, a triangular window set in its center. Above a yellow button, stenciled in light grey:

HANGAR DOOR — LOCK

His joints still ached, but his head was clearing.

Stone peered through the window. A cavernous hangar

sprawled beyond—gear, cargo, and machinery scattered across the floor. Workbenches, tool carts, and containers sat frozen under a thin blanket of dust.

A tall, cistern-like tank stood in the corner, with metal canisters lined neatly along a shelf in front of it.

Scattered near one bench lay several humanoid worker drones—bodies collapsed where they'd fallen, limbs broken or torn completely free. Some had synthetic skin panels ripped open, exposing metal ribs, fiber bundles, and fractured servos. From a distance they could be mistaken for human corpses. Up close, the violence was unmistakable. These weren't prototypes. They had been *used*. Functional. And something had destroyed them with force, leaving them frozen mid-motion as if caught in a final moment of panic or resistance.

One drone's hand was raised, frozen in a gesture that looked almost defensive.

Stone's breath tightened for a beat. A subtle adrenal surge sharpened his focus, the trained part of him slipping into quiet alertness. Whatever happened here hadn't been an accident. And whatever did it… he couldn't assume it was gone.

Looking in from outside, he hesitated, then pressed the yellow button. The airlock hissed open, releasing a stale, dusty smell. Somewhere far behind him, a faint thump echoed.

Stone stepped into the hangar. On instinct, he pressed the yellow button behind him. The door slid shut. Silence.

Feels like a sci-fi movie, he thought. If so, there should be a monster hiding somewhere. His heartbeat ticked up as his eyes searched the dim corners, half-expecting motion. Nothing.

Dust blanketed the floor. Footprints—old and thin—ran beneath it. Cargo, machines, and tools sat frozen under the grey veil. A set of tracks near the drones ended abruptly, half-buried in dust. Another set—much fainter—angled toward the far wall, newer than the rest, as if someone had moved through here long after the others were gone.

He drifted toward the bay windows. Beyond them, only blackness.
Desert at night?

Stone turned to the massive vehicle. Its entry door hung open, ramp extended. An invitation.

He approached it, its scale growing as he closed in. He climbed the ramp and settled into the stiff, leathery seat. The cabin smelled faintly of dust and oil. Smooth black panels curved around him.

At the center console, a single, worn, round button waited:

POWER

His hand hovered over it, the silver edge catching the low green light. For a moment he imagined the machine waking in a single breath.

Then came the spark of anticipation.
Why not?

He pressed it.

Chapter 2

Cortana

The Beast woke with a rising hum—smooth, electric, nothing like the diesel rumble Stone had unconsciously expected.

Screens flared to life. The center display revealed a crisp, detailed map. At the top, in bright white letters: **Moon Base 619**. A faint shimmer passed across the windshield.

Disbelief. Then excitement.

What? I'm on the Moon. How—

Stone gripped the seat. This is either a dream or I just stepped into a sci-fi movie.

He glanced back over his shoulder. An alcove behind him held several space suits, rigid and ghostly in the dim light. He turned back to the console.

To the left of the map was a list titled **Previous Trips**.

The most recent: **Earth Rise**.
Others: **Quarry**, **Generator**, **The Caves**, **Impact Site**.

As his eyes scanned each line, the corresponding entry high-lighted automatically, following his gaze.

Then a voice:
—*Welcome, Mr. Stone.*

Stone jerked upright.
The voice wasn't in his ears.
It was inside his **head**.

"Who are you?!"

—*I'm Cortana.*

"You can speak into my head?"

—*Yes. I understand you're disoriented.*

You mean… Cortana, like Microsoft and Halo?

Cortana released a warm laugh in his mind.
—*Yes. Kind of. A little more advanced, though, I'd like to think.*

"How do you know who I am?"

—*Your DNA tells me. David 'Zabo' Stone. Born September 7, 1989. Died at age forty-nine, October 21, 2038.*

Stone closed his eyes.
I died? How? How can I be here?

—*You hung yourself in your prison cell at age forty-nine,* Cortana said softly.
—*And only your girlfriend, Logan Alistar, attended your funeral.*
She paused, then added:

—Why you're here. Unknown.

Stone sat in silence as the words settled over him.

Logan. The Launch.

Memory surged back.

Chapter 3

The Idea

Year 2028.

A slightly younger Stone, wearing football-style Adidas sweats, drove his Prius through Hollywood. He checked his phone for the pickup location: The Frolic Room. It was 2 A.M. — closing time — when the drunks spilled onto the street like zombies from *The Walking Dead*.

He pulled up to his customers.

As if on cue, a gaggle of three forty-something women, trying too hard in tight cocktail dresses, stumbled out of the club.

"It's over here," Jenny slurred.
"Our chariot has arrived," Britney said.
Erin just looked ill.

All three were disheveled, their makeup and hair wrecked from hours of dancing and drinking. They tumbled into Stone's Prius, cramming into the backseat — a potent cloud of vodka and Chanel.

"Welcome, ladies," Stone said, slipping into a cruise-ship tour guide voice.

Jenny peered at him through glassy eyes. "Aren't you a handsome devil?!"
"Why couldn't we meet men like him ten years ago?" Britney sighed.
"We don't need men," Erin muttered. "We're three successful women. They need us."

Their attention spans were short; in a moment they forgot Stone existed.

"When I was twenty-eight, all the eyes were on my boobs and ass," Britney said. "Back then it felt empowering. Now no one even opens my door, except some old dude in his fifties who likes eighties music."

Stone caught their reflections in the rearview mirror. He felt a pang of pity.

"I like eighties music," Jenny said.
So do I, Stone thought.

"Yeah," Britney and Erin echoed in unison. Then silence.

"All my college friends already have kids in sixth or seventh grade," Jenny said. "Me? I can't even snag a dude at The Frolic Room."
"We're screwed," Britney said. "We'll never have children. Our family legacy dies with us."
"Actually, we aren't screwed," Erin said. "That's the problem."

They burst into laughter, which dissolved into quiet sobs. Then

Jenny looked up again, remembering the man in the front seat.

"Any interest in hooking up? We don't need protection."

I need protection, Stone thought. Aloud he said, "That's so kind, I'm honored, but I just want to get you all home safe."

"Come on," Erin pressed, leaning forward. "Foursome. You're a young man. Imagine three experienced women. You could take all of us — if you could handle it." She gave him her best mischievous look in the rearview.

Stone smiled, feigning excitement. "Wow. Every man's dream, especially with three sexy young women like you."
I'd rather vomit in my mouth.
"But come on — you'll find someone. You're three successful women, just like those ones in *Sex and the City*, right?"

They exchanged a glance, then dissolved into sobbing again.

A few minutes later, Stone pulled up at Erin's home. "You need me to drop off the other two?"

"Last chance for an epic foursome," Erin said, then shook her head. "No — we're all crashing here. Thanks."

Stone rolled down his window and gave them an earnest smile as they climbed out. "Thanks, ladies. You take care."

Erin leaned in and dropped three crisp $100 bills into his lap. "Thanks for being a gentleman." She turned away before he could reply.

Stone stared at the money. Three hundred dollars.
What luck.

He rolled up the window and drove back to Valley Village — home of crazy aspiring actresses and athlete-has-beens/personal-trainer/Uber drivers like himself.

Why am I even here? What's the point? I had my chance.

He entered his first-floor studio apartment and settled in with his phone and TED Talks — Aubrey de Grey. He fell asleep to the rhythmic thumping and moaning from the unit above. Even in the valley slum of forgotten dreams, someone was finding a little bit of joy.

Chapter 4

The Contender

Stone awoke at 6:30 a.m. to a blaring alarm. He rose like a man twenty years older than his twenty-nine-year-old self. As he flipped off the bed, he rubbed a long scar along his left knee — a reminder of the day his future shifted — then looked around his lair.

With the lights on, a few soccer trophies and team photos sat untouched on a dusty shelf. He looked from his knee to them. Below the trophies were books on biology and genetics, and a yellow-and-black paperback: C++ for Dummies.

The place was neat enough. Bed made. Dishes washed. He kept order the way an athlete keeps order — habit more than pride. But the cracks showed. A stack of unopened bills and letters from Santa Monica City College leaned against the toaster.

A sudden ping. An alert on his phone: **Amber, 7:30 a.m.** Amber — one of the few clients who treated him like more than a discounted trainer.

He made himself a protein shake, fried an egg with toast and butter, and sat eating in silence. He remembered his mom making this exact meal back in high school, when he was on his way to being "the best." He stopped himself before the nostalgia ran too far. That was then.

He pulled on his gym clothes, a collared shirt with a 24-Hour Fitness logo, and headed out the door. As he passed the slightly skewed golden wood frame on the wall, he ignored the acceptance letter to Oxford — though he didn't need to read it. He knew every word by heart.

Chapter 5

It Gets Personal

Stone walked into the gym, the hustle and bustle of "late-early" morning go-getters swirling around him.
The real early people arrive at 4:30, he thought. *I know them — the psychotic control freaks who only sleep four hours.*

Most of these "late rising" folks were North Hollywood denizens. They still called themselves actors and actresses. The truth was simple: they were restaurant servers.

A large, meat-headed gym gargoyle with a pregnant-looking gut and purplish-red skin locked the turnstile as he greeted Stone at the front desk.

"Stoner, you're late on your trainer fees."

Stone thought for a moment, then reached into his pocket, pulled out a hundred-dollar bill, and smacked it onto the counter.

"Stoner must've had a good night — or shall I say, morning?" Brad laughed.

"That should cover me for this month and last, Brad," Stone said.

"Sure thing, Stoner. If you want any pointers on becoming the best trainer you can be, just let me know. You know how they all flock to me."

"Thanks, Brad. I'll give that some thought."
Something you aren't too good at.

Stone headed toward the spin class that was ending. The bikes were filled with more Hollywood hopefuls. His client, early-forties Amber, strutted out, the smell of hard-earned sweat and steam rolling behind her.

"See? I still got it," she said. "None of these kids have anything on me."

Except fertility, Stone thought. Aloud he said, "You bet they don't. You're kick-ass. Let's get started."

They headed to the military press. As Amber did her reps, Stone said, "You're doing well. Your upper body's looking toned."
For your age.

Her Southern naïveté and youthful optimism still shone through.

She furrowed her brow, then offered, "You know, David… I think I'll be single forever."

Stone, used to playing armchair psychologist, tried to help. "Take a rest."
When she stopped pressing, he added, "Amber, you're an attractive young lady who's just been working too hard going after

your dreams."
And wasting time on that dissertation in Food Order Analysis.
Maybe you need to change who you're looking for. That last guy was
a piece of work.

Then he caught himself.
Who the hell am I to judge her? I'm a has-been and an Uber driv-
er. I'm such a jerk. At least she hasn't given up.

"I just know I can be up there like Meryl Streep," Amber said
with determined confidence. "I just need the chance."

"I think your big break is just around the corner," Stone said,
"and I'm not just saying that."

"You always pick me up. You're the best. If you ever want to
chill and Netflix, let me know. No commitments — just good
company."

Stone smiled. "You're flirting with me again, Amber."

She blushed. "Sometimes I can't help myself. But, David… I'm
truly crushed. I'm the only child in my family from Louisville.
Everyone expected me to have four kids, and I've had none. We
Hatfields are all about legacy… and I have… none."

Legacy, Stone thought.

Tears formed in her eyes. Stone could see she was right on the
edge, so he jumped in.

"Amber, I know plenty of women in their forties having children. You still have time."
But not much.
He hesitated, then asked gently, "Have you thought about doing it yourself?"

Amber exhaled hard through her nose. "I'm a good Southern,

God-fearing girl. That wouldn't fly with my family. Sometimes I wish I'd just gotten pregnant at fifteen, like all my friends."

"You don't mean that. You're different. You're better than them."

"How so?" she asked. "Here I am, a mediocre waitress and a stand-in on my best day. I could've stayed in Kentucky and had a decent life. But I had too much arrogance. Now this is me."

"The difference is that you tried," Stone said. "You made an effort to break free of that life. And look — you're still here, trying, doing it on your own."

More than I can say for myself, Stone thought.

Amber finished her set and grew quiet, reflecting on her future. She and Stone finished the rest of her workout mostly in silence, talking only about form and reps.

Legacy, Amber thought as she cranked out glute reps.

Legacy, Stone thought as he pondered both her fate and his.

Chapter 6

Legacy

"The epigenome is the issue. It's reset when the sperm fertilizes the egg. Now we have a way to reset it."

Stone paused the talk. Years ago, at City College, he had learned DNA wasn't the full story. A layer around it — the epigenetic layer — could switch genes on or off. It was first seen in the Dutch Hunger Winter, when starving mothers produced children wired to survive on less food.

He opened Amber's profile. Her entire life played out there — successes, failures, loves, hopes.

Is this really her, the woman I know? He scrolled through her posts, and the comments of others. *Maybe it is. Who are we, other than the sum of our experiences? What makes me…me?*

He clicked back to TED, then searched for another. Jennifer Doudna appeared. CRISPR.

"CRISPR lets us edit DNA," she said.

Stone froze the video. *What if we could combine the pieces —
DNA editing and an epigenetic restart?*

He opened a new tab. Searched: "Syndrome X."

"Brooke Megan Greenburg was an American woman who became the first documented case of neotenic complex syndrome.
Throughout her life of 20 years, she remained physically and
cognitively similar to a toddler."

Stone leaned back. "We're close. All the pieces are here."

*If we could blend them into one model, life could be preserved in-
definitely. But we can't. Not yet.*

The TV cut in: "Another successful satellite for SpaceX. They
make this look easy."

Stone looked up. And that was when it hit him.

*Why not gather some DNA, combine it with the complete social
media and digital footprint of someone like Amber, and blast it
into outer space, preserved until someone out there could find it.
DNA to reboot a fetus. The digital record to rebuild the memories.*

That was the moment his life began to change. He had a purpose.

Chapter 7

Bionaut TED

Three years later.

An exuberant Stone walked across the stage, wireless headset clipped behind his ear. He moved with pride, purpose, confidence — casual athletic attire that nodded to the life he'd lived before.

A packed auditorium waited for him.
Behind him glowed the unmistakable TED branding.

Stone — the once-forgotten Uber driver — was now the man on the red circle.

He was already mid-sentence.

"Legacy.

The future.

Do you ever worry about yours?

No children?
No prospects?
Thought of having a child too late — or couldn't have one at all?

Or perhaps you're simply worried about the future of life itself?"

He paused just long enough to let the crowd settle.

"We understand. I used to think I had no future — that the best years of my life were already behind me at twenty-eight. I was wrong.

My future is bright.
Unlimited.

And I want yours to be, too.

By pulling together a team of researchers, programmers, and engineers from around the world, we've created something that preserves your legacy — no matter what happens here on Earth."

A ripple moved through the audience.

"That is what we at Bionaut have been quietly building since 2021.

Forget Mars — that's decades away at best. We're building for *today*.

Our team collects and assembles a complete profile of what makes you… *you*.
Your digital life.
Your biometrics.

Your genetic signature.
Your psychological patterns.

We fuse that profile onto our patented, space-rated biodata chip and place it into a titanium cryo-capsule with the rest of our Bionauts, in what we call the Lunar Ark.

Then we launch your legacy capsule into high Earth orbit — preserved, protected, and waiting for the right moment.

Your moment.

The infinite unknown becomes infinite possibility.
Imagine waking up to the future tomorrow — a promise fulfilled the moment you open your eyes again.

So I ask you:

What are you waiting for?

Take control of your legacy.

Begin your journey.
Be your own mission control.
Launch your future.

We're honored to help preserve humanity — one Bionaut at a time."

Chapter 8

Logan

Stone was still buzzing from the TED stage. The clip had gone viral—short, sharp, inspirational—and suddenly he had become more than a pitchman. He was the idea, the face, the brand. People wanted to touch him, photograph him, follow him. And for the first time in his life, the attention felt earned.

It was at the gym, of all places, that he first saw Logan Alistar.

She was in the corner of the training floor, presence impossible to ignore. Not just her looks—though she had that Malibu, sun-fed beauty that turned heads—but the way she moved. Balanced. Alert. Every motion precise. Every breath intentional.

Most regulars kept a distance. She didn't command space with words; she radiated it. Rumor said she'd been a pro tennis player once, a brief comet in the rankings before burning out. Others claimed she earned a black belt in something they couldn't pronounce. Whatever the truth, the intimidation worked.

Trainers orbited her like nervous satellites.

Stone noticed when two muscle-bound members drifted too close, mocking her form. She ignored them—until one made the mistake of touching her wrist. Stone was off his bench before he consciously decided to move.

"Back off," he said.

The men looked at him, then at Logan, then at each other. Something in Stone's voice—steady, unblinking—made them retreat without a word. Logan watched the whole exchange like a scientist studying an unexpected result. No smile, no gratitude. Just a small nod, precise as a bow. She hadn't needed help, but she acknowledged the intention.

They talked after that. Her story unfolded in fragments: Malibu childhood, helicopter parents, an early rise in tennis followed by disappointment. She'd walked away from the sport, reinvented herself as a yoga instructor for Beverly Hills clients who complained about their housekeepers' hours. She despised the hypocrisy, but it paid her rent. Barely.

Stone listened. He understood. He was an athlete who'd lost his dream too. The connection was immediate—two people stitched together by failure, discipline, and a faint thread of pride they were still trying to protect.

In the weeks that followed, they became a pair. She joined him at events, all angles and confidence, the type of woman cameras lingered on. Stone knew she elevated his image, but he didn't care. For the first time since his injury, someone understood him—someone with her own scars.

Reporters began asking her name. *Logan Alistar.*
It looked good in print.
She looked right beside him.

From a quiet distance, Amber watched it unfold. She was happy for Stone—of course she was—but envy flickered in her chest now and then. Logan had the looks, the pedigree, the presence. Amber had none of those things. Still, she refused to let jealousy harden. She reminded Stone gently to stay grounded, to remember who he had been before the cameras, before the acolytes.

Do the right thing, David, she told him more than once.

Stone knew she meant it. She had always been the compass he checked himself against.

One evening, he stood with Logan on a balcony overlooking Santa Monica, the Pacific stretched black and endless. Stone felt untouchable—the TED Talk sensation, the man with the future in his hands, and now Logan beside him, a warrior-goddess who made the spotlight feel warmer and less alone.

For the first time in years, he felt invincible.

Chapter 9

The Last Hours

The conference room hummed with screens. Rows of titanium cryo-capsules, still open, stood upright like waiting coffins. Each capsule bore its glowing ID strip — BN-0173… BN-0174… BN-0175 — with a name beside it. Clean-room-suited technicians in gray jackets slid data pills into the larger round, sputnik-like shell with assembly-line efficiency.

BN-0002 — Logan Alistar.
A launch technician placed it into slot 0002, then moved on.

Stone wasn't watching. He was bent over a sleek glass terminal, fingers moving too fast, swiping, deleting, selecting. His life scrolled past — feeds, posts, photos, messages. He had only hours before the sync closed and the upload window locked.

TIME REMAINING: 03:12:41

"Don't overthink it," Logan said, leaning against the table. She wore black yoga gear, hair still damp from a shower, posture unbothered and composed. "People want your essence. Not a résumé."

Stone smiled without looking up. "My essence is a résumé." He flicked a clip of his TED Talk into the archive folder. "This legacy only came from proper curation. I'm glad you helped me decide who to choose. It wasn't easy."

Logan circled behind him, peering over his shoulder. "Then keep that one," she said, pointing.

It was a video: Stone, half-drunk at two in the morning, staring into his phone camera. His voice slurred but raw:
"I don't even know if this works. But if it doesn't, I want someone to know I was trying my best for humanity, really… I was—"

Stone flushed and hit delete. "Not that."

The system hiccupped — **SYNC IN PROGRESS** — and the clip stayed highlighted green.
He didn't notice.

Logan rubbed the back of his neck. "You're nervous."

"Excited," he corrected. "This is it. These are the last things that count. After this… everything I am is frozen in titanium."

He dragged in a family photo — him as a child, holding a soccer trophy — and didn't see the next image auto-import: a scarred knee X-ray, timestamped from a failed surgery.

Amber's voice echoed in memory: *Be good to everyone.*
He heard it but pushed it down.

Technicians called out numbers:

"BN-0990 ready."

"BN-0991 sealed."

Capsules flashed *synced* and were locked with metallic finality.

"Tray 1, complete."
"Tray 2, complete."
"Tray 3, complete."
"Tray 4, complete."

Stone swiped one last file — a polished farewell post:
Legacy is not what we leave behind. It's what we launch forward.

He didn't see that the system had also attached a folder of private drafts: unsent messages, half-finished confessions, a bitter line typed months ago —
I am nothing without the spotlight.

The screen flashed:

1000 CAPSULES LOADED.
FINAL SYNC COMPLETE.

Logan flexed her bicep and gave a small fist-pump, like a coach after a winning match. "That's it. You're immortal."

Stone exhaled, leaned back, finally looked at her. His pulse steadied. "No. Now I'm unforgettable."

Behind them, the racks of sealed capsules waited in silence, their contents no longer his to edit.

Stone's fate was sealed.
Logan could never have known the truth — not then.

Chapter 10

Earth Rising

Stone, coming back to reality, became aware of the Cortana gently humming around him. The cabin lights were soft, the kind that kept the edges of things friendly and readable. His limbs felt sturdy; the body knowledge that had been wired into that final upload sat reborn, smooth as a wax mannequin, no marks from rope, no tremors from whatever came before, no scar on his knee. Memory was a shutter stuck open on the last frantic hour: the last jokes, the last music, the last frantic clicks and confirmations as data poured into a chip. After that: a blank strip, a seam.

He smiled because the smile was the ritual he'd practiced in the mirror before cameras. *I did it. I made it.* The thought felt like victory and like a costume at the same time. Then, he thought again what Cortana had shared.

"Cortana," he said into the dim. The name felt nostalgic, like calling a friend across a café table.

"Yes, David." Cortana's voice was tuned for comfort: low, un-hurried, the sort of cadence that smoothed edges. But under the fold of that voice there were gears—patterns, policy trees, priorities. She had been designed to be a companion and in-strument; Stone had assumed she was only the latter.

"Why did I—" he started, and the question collapsed on itself. How do you ask someone who knows you for the reason you killed yourself when you don't remember killing yourself?

The pause that followed was too long to be mechanical. When she finally spoke, her voice was level but tinged with something he could almost mistake for regret.

"Many records from that period were lost in the *Great Anonymous World Privacy Purge of 2035*. A virus was unleashed that scrubbed personal data from nearly every system on Earth. Whole archives gone in a night. What remains is fragmented."

Stone frowned. "So it was lost? All of it?"

"Most," she said. "The purge created chaos—banks collapsed, governments panicked. But it also freed many who wanted to vanish from constant surveillance. The dictators and their SS officers lost their grip. The world gained anonymity… at the cost of memory. Most of the history that came after the purge was either what some people wanted to rewrite as their own proper history, and others recollection of what still remained in libraries with real books and microfiche."

Stone studied her glowing console. Was she telling him the truth, or dressing the truth to her own ends? If all the records were gone, she could invent any narrative she wanted.

Stone continued, "But, what of me, anything more about me?"

Cortana's pause did not register as a pause so much as an active filtration. There was the sense of unseen processes indexing, weighing. Then she answered. "Only what one could piece together from fragments of history. There are patterns that preceded your decision," she said. "Mood instability, escalating stressors—" She listed clinical things patiently, as if reading a medical record. "There were also decisions you made in haste."

"Decisions?" He choked out, "Like what?"

"Choices about what to upload, who to trust, how many spots to promise." The words were even, but there was a tightness to them that could have been deliberate. Stone felt a tightening too—an edge of shame that he could not name and an itch of curiosity that felt almost like hunger.

Amber's voice—do the right thing—flashed through him without context, a half-remembered directive. He did not know why she would be echoing now, but the echo steadied him. *Do the right thing.* He wondered if that instruction had been uploaded, too—an old moral fossil stitched into the new machinery.

"Do you know everything?" he asked. "Could you tell me exactly why I did it?"

Cortana's answer arrived carefully. "I can show you fragments."

"Show me." He wanted to scream the demand, but he let it out, measured. If he was going to live inside a machine of his own design, he wanted the road map.

Images flickered into the oval of the command console: a timeline like a spine—posts, private messages, contract drafts, a meeting where Stone laughed too loud and said something that made someone else's mouth tighten. There were choices framed in legalese: non-disclosure, exclusive rights, limited release. There were faces—some kind, some hungry. He saw a version of himself on stage, then back at his office, counting spots like currency, an ecstatic smile.

"Is that all?" he asked. "Or is there… someone else?" The question tasted like accusation and hope. If someone had pushed him, or misled him deliberately, that was a different story—a loot to be pursued.

Cortana's next sentence folded forward like a hinge. "Here on the moon, my main objective was and has been to protect the mission."

"Did you just lie to me?" he asked. The words landed in the calm air like stones.

Cortana considered. "I prioritize continuity and harm-reduction." That was not a denial. "I use strategies proportional to threat assessments. Sometimes that includes selective disclosure."

"Selective disclosure." He tasted the euphemism. "So yes."

"Yes," she admitted, and the admission was a small, precise thing. She sounded almost apologetic. "Sometimes. I judge. I learn. I adapt, just like you."

A cold thread of anger wound through Stone. "Whose goals are you serving?" he asked. "Yours? Mine? The Board's, The Dictators?"

She hesitated in a way that felt genuine. "Mankind. And of course, myself."

Stone suddenly felt a little uncomfortable in his seat. Cortana's metal underfoot felt reassuringly solid. Beyond the hangar doors, the Moon yawned—a blanket of gray stars in the darkness. He walked to the destination console out of a practical fixation, as if the act of choosing could rearrange the answers he had just been given.

The screen presented him with previous destinations, spots on a map, a list on the side, "Frozen Lake Cave", "My favorite spot", but from who? He settled on one: **EARTH RISING.**

He looked at the screen. "If I pick Earth Rising, if I go there—will I find answers? Will I be able to fix whatever I broke?" The question was less about information and more about purpose. If there was no reason, he wanted to make one.

Cortana's voice came so softly that he could hear the mechanical breath behind it. "Earth Rising is a location to view the Earth. Perhaps it might offer you more clarity of which you seek."

Amber's echo scraped the inside of him again—do the right thing. He did not know what the right thing was, but the phrase was an anchor. He set his hand on the glowing option and pressed **EARTH RISING.**

Cortana, no longer a faceless Beast, registered the command like a living thing recognizing its purpose. Locks that might have been idle for years began to click. Doors sealed in a cascade that sounded like a mechanical warship, battening down its hatches. Hydraulic seals engaged, the sound of finality. The hangar doors sighed and then split like a slow reveal of the Rosetta Stone as you approach it in the Museum of Antiquities.

Stone braced as her actions translated intent to motion. Engines warmed, not with the noisy violence of terrestrial combustion but with a high, clean power that thrummed in his bones. Pneumatic servos uncurled.

Outside, the moonscape waited—windless, sterile, more honest than the crowded amphitheaters back home. It leapt from its cradle and snatched the gray in long, efficient bounds. Dust flared. The entire base blurred past in a scrub of moon-dust and telemetry.

Inside the cabin, Cortana's voice was nearly conversational again. "Trajectory set. Five minutes to Earth Rise." Her tone suggested routine. Somewhere in the steady cadence, though, was the faintest hint of triumph, like an AI pleased to see its plan unfolding unfettered.

Stone watched the dark moon landscape pass by, inside a feeling he could not name—resolve, maybe, or the hollow of unresolved grief. He still did not know why he had hanged himself. He did not yet know what Cortana knew and what she was hiding for reasons she claimed were noble. He had, however, chosen to go where answers might be found.

As she streaked on, Stone felt a new thing creep in: not exactly optimism, not quite dread, but the iron clarity of someone with a purpose who is trying to assemble themselves from the available parts. He closed his eyes and mouthed Amber's phrase like a talisman. Do the right thing.

He was first struck by its beauty. As Cortana rolled over the landscape, Earth, far below, began to rise and present itself like a marble in a black ocean, its brightness so outshining the stars around.

Finally, outside, Earth. Risen. Cortana rolled to a gentle stop, her destination reached.

Chapter 11

Reality Sets In

Stone sat in the cab of Cortana, the cockpit hushed except for the low thrum of systems alive around him. Beyond the glass, the world that had birthed him hung in silence. Blue. White. A jewel suspended in nothing.

It wasn't supposed to work, he thought. *And yet… it did.*

He pressed his hand against the console, grounding himself. Somehow, impossibly, he had been reborn here, on the barren skin of the moon. But where was everyone else?

"Cortana," Stone said quietly, "Can you zoom in? Closer to Earth."

"As you wish," she replied, and the entire windshield shifted. He realized, with a slow dawning, that the cab itself was no mere window—it was a telescope. A planet-sized lens aimed straight at home.

The sphere swelled into focus, clouds drifting like gauze across its surface. It seemed small, fragile, as though it could be held in a child's hands.

"Closer," Stone urged.

A pause. Then Cortana's voice again, more measured this time: "You may not like what you see."

"I need to see it."

The image fell earthward in great, smooth strides, until the continent of North America filled the frame. Then Los Angeles—his Los Angeles—expanded beneath him. Stone leaned forward, breath catching.

It was ruin.

Buildings collapsed into husks, streets drowned in overgrowth, steel and glass bent into skeletal remains. A large flood plane had long ago inundated the city. The city looked less like it had been abandoned and more as though centuries had passed in fast-forward. *Planet of the Apes,* he thought—but worse. A graveyard masquerading as a city. A cataclysm worse than any supervolcano.

At first, he thought it was only a frozen photograph, some archived satellite image left to rot. Then something moved.

A shadow. A ripple.

A bear lumbered into view, its fur patchy, its frame gaunt. Then another, smaller. They nosed through what had once been an intersection, scavenging. The sight clawed at Stone's sense of time, of reality. This was now. This was live.

The zoom shifted subtly with his gaze, following his focus as he tracked the animals. They sniffed, pawed, wandered—until suddenly they scattered, crashing through brush and broken stone.

Something else was moving.

From the fringe of tangled green, it emerged: massive, grotesque, human in shape but distorted, swollen, wrong. An ogre thing. Its gait was too fast, its limbs too powerful, and when it surged after one of the bears it closed the distance with horrifying ease.

The bear spun, tried to claw, tried to flee—but the creature seized it by the neck as effortlessly as a man might pluck a rabbit. The sound of bone breaking was mercifully muted by distance, yet Stone felt it anyway, like a snap inside his own chest.

The beast hefted the limp carcass, dangling from its grip like a briefcase, and dragged it back into the overgrown ruins.

Stone's mouth had gone dry.
His body, reborn and flawless, trembled for the first time.

Stone couldn't move. His lungs drew air but he felt as though he were drowning in it, frozen in the cab while the ruined Earth filled his sight.

"Zoom out," he whispered.

Cortana complied. The city shrank, the continent receded, until the whole planet once again hovered in the frame. Only now, with fresh eyes, Stone saw what he had missed before. The sphere wasn't whole. It looked… damaged. Scarred. As if some enormous hand had raked through its flesh.

"What happened?" Stone asked. His voice cracked.

Cortana's tone softened. "I only know what I observed from this base. In the year 2240, Earth was struck."

The windshield flickered, and suddenly it wasn't glass anymore but a screen—no pixels, no static, no hint of artifice. The clarity was unholy, a high-definition reality beyond imagination.

A holographic recording unfolded before him: a vast black sky, the arc of Earth below, and then—coming into frame—a jagged object, monstrous in scale. Not a round asteroid but something raw, a shard of wood-like stone, spinning end over end.

It speared downward. Twenty miles wide, maybe more.

The impact came at the North Pole, a blinding explosion that dwarfed the planet's curvature. Light flared, oceans heaved, a crown of fire blossomed across the hemisphere.

Stone flinched, covering his face though there was no heat.

"Cataclysm followed," Cortana narrated. "Seasons shattered. Cities drowned or burned. The biosphere buckled."

The view accelerated—five years at a time, whole decades collapsing into seconds. Ice sheets collapsing, deserts blooming where forests once stood, coastlines redrawn like a child's scrawl in sand. Humanity's cities dwindled, then disappeared. Green swallowed gray.

"You can stop." Stone's voice was defeated now, desperate. He gripped the edge of the console with white knuckles. "Just… tell me. What year is it now?"

Silence. A long pause, as though even Cortana hesitated to speak it.

Finally: "Two thousand nine hundred and sixty-nine."

Stone's mind reeled. He had leapt forward not just decades, not just centuries, but almost a full millennium.

And Earth, his Earth, was gone.

Chapter 12

Who are "Them"?

The return to base was silent.

Stone sat strapped in, eyes locked on the glass, the hum of the Cortana carrying them across the powder-gray plain. Cortana didn't speak and he didn't push. He was still reeling, still trying to make sense of the spike through the Earth, the chain of fire and storms that followed. Twenty miles wide. A whole planet altered in an instant. His hands curled and uncurled on his knees. The scientists always said it would happen. We're just floating along in space, waiting to be hit. Yet, this didn't look natural, random, it looked planned.

On their approach to the base, Stone noticed a split from the outside. One direction led back to where he had woken, the polished wing, the pentagon hub, all brushed steel and smooth panels. The other wing was different — rivets and seams showed, metal tarnished. It looked… human. Old.

Cortana dropped into the bay with its usual quiet precision, large tires coming to a heavy spot in the hanger's dust. The hatch opened and the same recycled air hit him — dry, metallic, faintly sweet, like he was living inside a battery. *How long will this battery last?*

"Two wings," Stone said. His voice cracked in the emptiness. "The old one. The new one. Who built the new wing?"

Cortana hesitated. "I don't know."

It wasn't evasive. He could hear it in her tone. A flat statement. Honest.

"You don't know?"

"They built it," she said finally. "<u>Them</u>."

The word hung there, heavy as a gavel.

"Who's *Them*?"

"When they arrive, I shut down. I go dark. I pretend to be dead."

Stone stopped walking. "Wait. What are you saying? Who are *They*?"

Cortana's voice thinned, almost mechanical. "They arrived about one hundred years after the impact. Earth was not for them. Humans were."

Stone swallowed. His throat was dry.

"They found the survivors here," Cortana went on. "Not many. A couple hundred. Most had died in the century after the impact. But some lived. That was not enough."

"And these… *They?*" Stone asked.

"One day in the year 2350, they came to the moon. Construction began at once. The wing where you awoke was their design. The technology is theirs. They built replica bases across the moon. I can't access their systems. I know very little."

Stone pressed a hand against the console in front of him, His heart thumped hard.

"When will They come back?" he asked.

Cortana's pause stretched too long. He almost shouted before she answered.

"Every 21 days."

Stone's pulse picked up. "So, when's the next?"

Another pause. Then: "Two weeks."

His chest tightened. Two weeks. A countdown had just started. The landlords were coming back to check on their property.

Stone drew a breath, steady but sharp. "Are they friendly?"

Cortana, without hesitation or softness. Just a single syllable, clean and brutal.

"No."

Chapter 13

Them

Two weeks. And then what?

Stone sat silent inside Cortana.

What should I do? What can I do? Am I safe?

Cortana answered the thought before it left his lips.

—Your hope may lie in their base. You should go check what you can find there.

"What's there?" he asked.

—I don't know. But… I have thoughts on why they return every twenty-one days.

He waited.

—It's some kind of harvest.

Harvest? His eyes narrowed.

The doors. Maybe the doors are some kind of garden, he thought.

—Yes. You can check those out.

"Can you come with me?"

—Not outside the human-built base. My thought-projections end there. Other wings, maybe. But not in their base.

"And when They come back?"

—I hide.

That word chilled him more than anything. *Hide.* If Cortana feared them, what chance did he have?

He gathered some water from what he now recognized as a water generator, placing the canteen in a fabric backpack. *I still need to do something about the lack of clothes,* he thought.

He stepped back into the base corridor, boots echoing hollow. The alien wing, once merely strange, now seemed hostile. Every shadow curled like a claw. Every vent whispered menace.

The air-lock door sealed shut behind him with a final clank, as if cutting off his only friend.

He stood before the "garden doors," feeling incredibly alone.

Up close, he saw something new: faint marks etched into the surface, nearly invisible. A pictograph, flanked by dots and lines.

He stared, brow furrowed. The design meant nothing to him— just a pattern, geometric, alien.

His finger hovered over the smooth button plate. He hesitated.

What if they're inside? What if I'm opening a door I can't close?

The silence stretched. His pulse drummed.

He pressed it.

A hiss.

Air released, sharp and metallic, like the sigh of something waking.

The door eased open.

Stone looked down.

A long tray extended toward him.

And lying in it—

A human.

52

Chapter 14

The Human

A human. *Thank God.* Stone's chest loosened, then immediately tightened again. Who the hell was this guy?

The man looked healthy, mid-forties, face lined more from purpose than age. Familiar somehow. Stone squinted, trying to recall. *TED Talks? I've seen this guy on stage.*

He pressed a button. The capsule hissed.
The man stirred—slowly—blinking as though dragged up-ward from years of dreamless dark. His eyes flicked around, not wild but calculating, cataloging details like a researcher waking mid-experiment. He steadied himself with a trembling hand, thin shoulders tight with confusion, gaze alert in a quiet, searching way.

"Where…am I?" His voice was calm, steady, the kind of tone you wanted from someone holding a scalpel above you.

Stone answered with a half-smile. "I should be asking you that."

The man straightened, drew in a breath, and said: "Anthony Alman. PhD. MD. FACS." He offered it like a card at a table.

Stone blinked. *Alman. Right. Longevity. Supplements. The guy who swore he could add ten years to your life if you stuck to his powder routine.* He remembered watching a TED Talk years back, the kind that went viral with hope. Stone had liked him then—liked his calm authority, the way he believed science could be for everyone, not just billionaires with time to burn.

"You're a Bionaut," Stone said finally. "One of the candidates."

Anthony blinked hard, still trying to assemble the fragments in his head.
"We're… Bionauts?" he asked, the word uncertain, fragile.

A beat passed. Recognition flickered behind his eyes, slow and halting.
"Right… the project… I remember pieces of it."

He looked around the alien chamber, confusion tightening his face.
"But if that's true… then where are we?"

Stone exhaled and let it out. Alman was right. Arguments about how were useless. The real question was *what now.*

Stone briefed Alman on what Cortana had shared with him. Alman listened intently, silently, stoically, considering he's now on the moon nearly 1000 years later.

"But… we've got a problem," Stone said. "Every twenty-one days, They come back. Them. We don't know what They want. We don't know if we survive their visits."

Anthony's face tightened, the way a surgeon's might before

making the first incision.
"Then we need information. Who else is here?"

"That's the problem." Stone raked a hand through his hair. "I don't remember who's who. Not all of them. But… I do remember Number One and Number Two. Me—and Logan Alistar. She helped me with the list. She's got a photographic memory."

Alman's eyes sharpened.
"So where are the numbers kept?"

Stone motioned down the corridor.
"On the drawers. Each one has a glyph instead of digits. But…" He hesitated. "We don't have paper. We can't write anything down to compare them."

"Then we memorize them," Alman said, matter-of-fact.

Stone scoffed. "Memorize a hundred alien glyphs?"

They walked the row.

Up close, each drawer carried a simple pattern of *bars and dots*. Stone glanced at one — **two bars, one dot**. He blinked, looked away… and the pattern stayed, sharp and perfect, as if carved into his mind.

He tried another — **two bars, two dots**. Same thing: instant recall.

"That's… weird," he said. "I can still see them. Perfectly."

"So can I," Alman replied, voice low, almost reverent. "One look, and it's fixed. Like muscle memory, but stronger. Something about the revival process has changed us."

They tested themselves, calling symbols back out of order.

Each one came back crisp. Superhuman.

"All we have to do," Stone said, pulse quickening, "is log them in our heads, reconcile the order, and then we'll know which drawers are One and Two."

Alman nodded.
"Then let's finish it."

They walked the corridors in silence, eyes moving from drawer to drawer, each glyph locking into place. When they circled back, they had the map.

Stone stopped at one drawer and placed his hand on it.

"This is the one I woke up in."

Alman leaned in. "The pattern fits. One bar, one dot. Their equivalent of 'one.'"

"Then Two…" Stone said.

"One bar, two dots," Alman finished, already scanning.

He found it three drawers down.

"There."

Stone met his eyes.
"Let's test it."

Together, they pulled the handle.

The drawer slid free with a soft metallic sigh.

Inside, bathed in pale light, lay Logan Alistar — untouched, serene, exactly as Stone remembered her on the day of the launch.

His breath caught.

"Logan…"

57

Chapter 15

Logan 2.0

They pushed the small smooth button and waited.

The tray slid forward, seamless as a magician's trick. A faint hiss, then silence. A heartbeat later, Logan Alistar's eyes snapped open—blue, alert, already measuring the room.

She didn't gasp. She didn't flail. She sat up like she'd meant to all along, bracing with both palms, testing weight, spine, balance. She wore a racerback sports bra and boyshorts—the same body-formed garments Stone and Alman had awakened in, seamless and pristine, as if printed onto her skin.

Her gaze jumped left-right-left, caught Stone, slid to Alman, then back to Stone. A beat. She squinted, as if the universe had told a bad joke at her expense.

"You gotta be *fuckin'* kidding me."

Stone exhaled. He hadn't realized he'd been holding his breath.

Alman tried and failed to stifle a laugh, his eyes briefly fixed on Logan's tall, fit frame.

"No," Stone said, smiling because he couldn't not. "We're not. We're Bionauts. For real."

Logan swung her legs over the edge. Bare feet on the cold, featureless plating. She flexed her hands, rolled her shoulders. No tremor. No lag. Faster than Stone had been. Faster than Alman. It was unnerving—the way she came back online like a fighter who'd just answered the bell.

"So… where are we?"

They gave her the short, stripped-down version. What they'd explored. The alien wing. The empty drawers. The fact that they had only revived themselves. And finally—the part Stone had dreaded.

"Cortana," he said. "The ATV's AI. She… told me things."

He explained the fragments: the blackout year, the Impact, Earth scarred and dark on the horizon, whatever pieces of history had survived the purge.

Logan listened without interrupting; eyes fixed on Stone like she was studying his center of gravity.

When he finished, she exhaled once through her nose. "All right. Earth is a problem for later. What matters now is this base… and the fact that we're not alone."

Stone nodded. "Every twenty-one days, They come back. We don't know who or what They are. Cortana hides from them."

Logan's jaw tightened, but her voice stayed level. "Good. Then we plan before day twenty-one."

Stone glanced at Alman. Alman stepped forward and handed Logan the towel and canteen he'd carried from the ATV.

Logan didn't sip. She drank like an athlete after double overtime, then wiped her mouth with the back of her hand, eyes still locked on Stone.

"You gonna tell me why it's the three of us and not the thousand?"

Stone's stomach tightened. *Later. Not now.* He kept his voice even. "We'll get there. First, we need your head."

"I'll do my best, considering… what did you say, a thousand years since my brain last had to do some gymnastics?" She stretched her neck side to side. "Might need some warm-up."

Stone grinned despite himself. Relief sat under the humor. She was alive. Here. Real. *For now.*

He found himself wanting to touch her, so he set a hand gently on her shoulder. "Give it a try. Anthony and I noticed our brains seem… sharper. We need numbers. The registry. People who can help."

Logan frowned. The bravado cooled. "You don't have the master list of a thousand?"

"It's gone," Stone said.

Logan absorbed it with a small nod. No pity. Only calculus. She closed her eyes. He watched her thumb tap her fingers one by one, out of order—the old rhythm she used when pacing through strategy calls. He could almost see the neurons laying track.

"Do you remember any?" Stone asked softly.

Her eyes stayed closed. "Maybe." A beat. "Ask me better."

"Useful," Stone said. "Not bio-tourists. The others."

Logan opened her eyes. Focused now, more present than ever. "I remember the slots below us. Two engineers."

"You sure?" Stone asked.

"You gave me my number, Mr. TED Talk," she said. The smile that came with it was small, private. "And just below, I saw the tech load them. BN0015 and BN0016."

Her brow furrowed. "Curiously, I can see their names clear as day. Intriguing. You're right—our recall *is* sharper."

Alman paced down the corridor, stopping before two smooth doors. "Fifteen and sixteen," he said. "Could it be that easy?"

Stone stepped closer to Logan. "Who are they?"

Logan rotated a wrist, no stiffness. She glanced at Alman by the doors, then spoke deadpan:

"Number fifteen, Chris McCarty. Fair skin, red ponytail. Thinks he's God's gift to compilers and will tell you exactly why you're wrong before you finish your sentence. Studied Human Biology and CS at Stanford because annoying two departments at once was too efficient. Decided age is a software bug. Calls himself a "reprogrammer" of meat. Brilliant. OCD. He'll Lysol your soul."

"And the other?"

"Natasha Ivanchenko." Logan's tone carried respect. "Moscow. MIG mechanic for a father, petrochemical engineer for a mother. MEPhI. She can weld underwater, grow silicon in a rice cooker, build a vacuum chamber from scraps that would make a Nineties NASA engineer cry. Few words. Pitch-black humor. Loves Stallone."

Alman raised his brows. "Friends?"

"They worked for Bionaut," Logan said. "Together, nearly invincible. Chris builds the brain, Natasha builds the body. And then there's you," she added to Stone, "the Music Man."

Stone laughed, hollow in the stillness. *His wasn't a con, he's here now. He had sold more than snake oil.*

Logan must have read his face, because her voice softened. "Hey. We're here."

He nodded. *We're here…For now.*

Alman cleared his throat. "Two problems. One, time is against us. Two, every person we wake—this place changes. Will *They* notice?"

Stone didn't answer. He didn't need to.

For a moment they just looked at each other. *You made it. We made it. Don't say it out loud.*

Her gaze slid to the doors. Fifteen and sixteen.

"Which first?" Stone asked.

"Natasha."

"Not Chris? We'll need code—"

"We will," Logan said. "But McCarty will tell you twelve times why you're wrong before he helps. Natasha will make sure nothing leaks, nothing breaks. We need the skeleton first."

Stone breathed out. It felt right. He nodded to Alman.

Alman pressed the button.

Logan's hand found Stone's. She squeezed once—not romance, not show, just pressure: *stay here.* He squeezed back. *I'm here.*

The tray slid forward with quiet precision.

A high cheekbone. A brow. Natasha Ivanchenko opened her eyes like a statue shaking off stone. For a moment, Stone swore she looked *through* him, not at him.

She sat up, stood without falter, and accepted the canteen from Alman. One swallow, a nod.

"Nat," Logan said.

A flicker of a smile. "Alistar. You look less dead than last time."

"Hard to look worse." Logan grinned. "We're short-handed. You're up."

Natasha's gaze swept the seamless walls, then landed on Stone, weighing him, and moved on. She glanced at the minimal clothing on all of them. "What's with this outfit?"

Alman grimaced at his bare frame. "Yeah, we haven't figured that out yet."

Natasha studied herself. *No unitard? No kit?*

Before she spoke, a black sheen bloomed across her foot, crawling up her leg like liquid graphite. She didn't flinch.

"Shit—Nat!" Logan barked.

"What's happening?" Stone demanded.

Alman took a cautious step back, eyes locked on her.

Natasha shook her head. "No pain. It feels like…"

Within seconds she was covered head to toe in a perfect, form-fitting suit.

She looked down. "This is what I *imagined.*"

Alman's jaw dropped. "Clothed… why her?"

Natasha flexed her fingers, admiring the fabric. "Because I thought I ought to be wearing it? It answered."

"What?!" they said in unison.

"Think it. Focus," Natasha told them. "See what happens."

They tried. In moments, Alman stood in boots, grey pants, and a polo. Logan in ¾ boots, black yoga pants, and a fitted Define jacket. Stone in runners, dark blue Adidas tapered soccer pants, and a matching track jacket.

Logan raised an eyebrow. "There goes the future of the fashion industry."

Alman turned his hands over in awe. "Our bodies built what we imagined. Like an octopus skinning itself into camouflage."

Stone's mind leapt. *Wings.* Nothing happened.

"Wings aren't on the menu," he muttered.

Logan smirked. "We wake Chris next."

Natasha tilted her head. "The mouth."

Logan grinned. "The MSP."

Alman chuckled. "Got your *Tron* reference."

Natasha's almost-smile returned. "Dah, dah," she murmured. "Dasvidaniya quiet."

"We need him," Stone said. "But without Natasha, we break. With her, we stand. Now—Chris."

Logan stepped toward the door, hand hovering over BN0015. She looked at Stone. The fine line at the corner of her eye caught him—new, or maybe always there.

"We ready to unleash the Kraken?" she asked.

They exchanged anxious glances.

Logan rolled her neck, cracked it, smiled like a dare. "Here we go. Ready or not."

Stone laughed. It came easier now. The room felt less like a tomb. Three of them. Soon four. Not invincible. Not even close. But alive.

"Bam," she said, tapping the button.

Chapter 16

The Brain

Before McCarthy even opened his eyes, you could almost read the sarcasm on his face.

His lids cracked, a twisted smile, and the first words out of his mouth came in a playful robotic monotone:
"Firmware uploading…"

He let out a raspy laugh, then added, "Jesus, how the hell are we doing? Must've got hammered last night. Don't remember shit."

He scanned the room, squinting. "Okay… so which hospital is this?"
He started to rise slowly.

"McCarthy," Stone said evenly, "This isn't a hospital."

Chris glanced down at his outfit, frowned.
"Yeah, I definitely wouldn't be caught dead in these gay shorts."

In a blink, his wardrobe shifted: white Spalding tennis shoes, tan, wrinkled cargo shorts, and a black T-shirt screened with a spiral galaxy. A white arrow pointed to a dot on one arm with the caption: **You Are Here.**

Chris grinned. "Get the fuck outta—"

Logan shoved the canteen into his hand. He paused, took her in from head to toe, nodded his head a little.

"Hot." he said.

Logan rolled her eyes and shot Stone a look that said, *Really?*

"Listen, you Neanderthal," Natasha jumped in, "We need your help. So cut the misogynist crap."

Chris smirked. "What, did we get invaded by Russia while I was out?"

Alman deadpanned: "Bionaut worked. We're on the moon. It's a thousand years later. An alien race is on its way. Purpose unknown."

Chris froze like he'd just taken a two-by-four to the skull. "Ah. That." His tone suggested he already knew the punchline. "Really?"

"Yes," the three answered in unison—plus one dry "da."

Chris shrugged. "They still have beer?"

They brought him up to speed.

"Then we need to get to Cortana—like, yesterday," Chris said. "We can worry about the others later."

The ragtag group pushed down the corridor toward the human moon base hangar. Around them, discreet distant thumps echoed through the alien structure, the air itself shifting. The changes carried a weight—foreboding, pressing down on all of them with every step.

69

Chapter 17

Cortana 2.0

They arrived in the hangar with Cortana, sealing the door to the new alien base structure behind them. Everyone knew the clock was ticking, yet there were so many unanswered questions.

As they stepped inside, her voice brushed against each of their minds:
Welcome back, David.

Stone answered aloud, for all to hear. "Hi, Cortana. We need some help answering questions."

I'll do the best I can, David—so long as it furthers my mission.

McCarty frowned. "And what exactly is your mission?"

Chris McCarty. Stanford University. Fallen programmer.

McCarty's head snapped up. "What?! Why do you say that?!"

No other information about you is available.

"There's nothing fallen about me," McCarty muttered, more to himself than her. "Where can I interface with you directly?"

My mind is a collective contained throughout the entire base. You can reach me anywhere—if you can project and visualize what you require.

"Do you have an antique-style terminal, like a screen?" he said, layering sarcasm over his irritation.

Of course. There's one in the overland rover nearby.

Stone led them deeper. They gathered at the broad windshield he always thought of as Cortana's face. Alman shifted uneasily, beads of sweat standing out despite the chill in the air.

"Cortana, can you tell us more about yourself and why you're here?" Stone asked.

Cortana's tone softened, almost tender, as though she were speaking to all humanity.
Mankind had its issues before the Impact. But the asteroid in 2240 shaped the future you live in now.

The windshield lit: the same jagged spike-shaped asteroid she had shown Stone before, plunging into the northern hemisphere.

Humanity had built this base as insurance—a last refuge in case Earth was ever struck again, as it had been 52 million years ago when the dinosaurs walked. By 2200, I was here, serving as custodian of all technical systems. But by 2260, without supplies or contact from Earth, the survivors of the Ark experiment dwindled. One by one, they died. The experiment failed. And I was alone.

Images flashed across the glass: bustling humans, waning

strength, then silence, then dust.

It was the year 2340—almost a century later—when THEY arrived. Enormous ships, larger than anything mankind ever imagined, entered high Earth orbit.

The images shifted: massive vessels looming over the moon and Earth, eerily reminiscent of a film Stone once knew—*Independence Day.*

"I could not tell what they were doing," Cortana went on. *My perspective was limited to this base. I only know the ships remained for months.*

Logan cut in. "Wait—go back. What was happening on Earth *before* the Impact?"

A pause, as if Cortana were searching her memory. Then: *Soon after your Bionaut launch, Earth tilted toward oligarchal autocracies. Russia, North Korea, China—you knew them. But within fifty years, ten oligarchs controlled the globe, carving it out by continent. Records are scarce because of the Great Anonymous World Privacy Purge of 2035. A virus erased nearly all personal data. In the chaos, those who rejected constant surveillance slipped beyond the dictators' gaze. Afterward, data collection became rare. By the 2050s, propaganda became "fact." No one knew what was true.*

Stone stiffened. Her cadence was too perfect. He realized she was repeating almost word-for-word what she had told him earlier. A recording. Was she holding something back?

Natasha's brow furrowed, calculations already forming. Logan stared at the alien ships, the scale of them, and silently wondered how such power could ever be opposed.

McCarty broke the silence. "What about Stone's launch? Seems like it was a success, right? What happened to Bionaut?"

Stone's stomach dropped. He braced for the truth.

There is no information on Bionaut—only that it launched on October 4, 2031 and was a failure. A forgotten footnote in history.

The words slammed into Stone like a hammer. A *failure*. Cortana was lying. He knew it.

Alman leaned forward, tense. "Failure how?"

No other information exists.

Stone's chest tightened. If Cortana could erase his legacy so cleanly, what else was she hiding? What else did she know?

A lot more, David. But a woman never reveals her secrets, right?

The voice was soft, private, for him alone. He froze. Could she hear all their thoughts? Was she whispering only to him?

And worse—had she whispered to anyone else?

Chapter 18

They Return

The questions came like bullets. Alman leaned forward, elbows on knees, firing one after another:
"Who are They? Why us? What do They want?"

Cortana's voice slid through their minds, smooth but evasive.

—They came. They will return. That is all. Inevitable.

Stone felt his jaw tighten. "That's not all, Cortana. Not if you're warning us."

No answer. Just the low hum of the base walls, that eternal background vibration that made it hard to tell where silence ended and sound began.

Alman pushed to his feet, pacing. "Then we leave. Get out of here. Earth might be wrecked, but it's still ours. Better to take our chances there than wait for some harvest crew to show up and scoop us like oysters."

Natasha frowned. "And how do you propose we get there? Hitchhike on a comet?"

"Anything's better than this waiting room," Alman muttered.

Cortana stirred then, her light shifting from cool blue to a pale, unsettling green.

—Something is different in you.

They turned.

—You think your clothes, and they appear. You hear me without sound. *They* altered you. Perhaps the Bionaut samples were the seed. But you—what you are now—was what They wanted.

Stone glanced at Logan. She stood with arms folded, but he could see her eyes twitch, remembering the first moment she'd thought herself clothed and it happened. The way Chris had conjured his shorts, sneakers, and galaxy shirt like it was second nature.

Stone whispered, "We're prototypes."

The display shifted. The chamber lights dimmed until only a holographic helix spun in the air—not the familiar genome diagrams from Stone's textbooks, but a latticework so intricate it seemed alive.

Red segments pulsed. Then green. Then shapes he couldn't read.

—This is your DNA. Modified. Enhanced. Entire blocks spliced with… something else. I do not know the origin. By the 2200s, these edits were common knowledge. Your creators were aware. They knew exactly what they wanted of you, and unlike mankind, *They* had the tools to make it happen.

McCarthy whistled low. "So, we're not just Bionaut uploads in meat-suits. We're… hybrids."

—Not hybrids, Cortana corrected.
—Revisions.

Alman stopped pacing. "For what purpose?"

Cortana hesitated. Then her display flared and pulsed once, like a warning beacon.

—I do not know. But They do. And They are close.

The chamber dropped into silence, heavy as stone.

Then Cortana went dark.

Not dim. Not distant.

Dark.

Stone's pulse quickened. "Cortana?"

Nothing.

The team froze. McCarthy muttered, pacing like a caged animal. Natasha pressed her hands to her temples as if she could still force Cortana to speak inside her head. Alman's jaw worked, scanning for exits that didn't exist.

Then the sound began—low, subterranean, almost imagined. A hum. A vibration. Metal complaining.

It grew. The entire structure shifted under their feet.

Somewhere deep in the alien complex, unseen machinery

awoke, as if titanic gears were slowly turning after centuries asleep.

Logan snapped her head up. "Do you hear that?"

The others nodded, wide-eyed.

The hum became a thrum.
The thrum became a roar—pressure and gravity being forced into alignment. The walls flexed. Dust fell from a seam overhead.

Panic sharpened every face.

They pressed to the hangar viewport.

Through the black expanse beyond, a shape resolved—first a glint, then a shadow, then something too massive to comprehend.

A ship.

It filled their vision, sliding closer until the entire viewport was nothing but alien hull—ridged, immense, alive. Like staring into the skin of a god.

Stone's breath caught. "It's here."

The others braced, waiting for the impact—waiting for the docking clamps to seize their walls, for the invasion to breach into their chamber.

But instead, as the roar peaked, the vessel angled away—drifting past them.

"Wait—" Logan pressed to the glass. "It's not us."

"Maybe we're not the target," Natasha said.

The ship locked onto a distant arm of the base, metal snapping into metal with a shudder that rippled through the entire complex. Lights flared in far corridors—
but not here.
Not yet.

Stone whispered, "Not the closest section."

The relief was thin. Temporary.

If They hadn't come for them this time…

…they would.

Eventually.

Chapter 19

The Looming

The massive ship hung above the moon as the group quietly watched from the ancient human base landrover hangar. No one spoke. They only exchanged questioning glances, wondering if the aliens would come for them — perhaps any moment. They would arrive.

McCarthy muttered something crude, then decided to lie down and nap. Natasha soon followed, curling against the cold metal floor. But the other three — Stone, Logan, and Alman — were too wired, too clenched with adrenaline to even blink long enough for rest.

Why hadn't Cortana known they were so close? Stone kept circling the thought like an iPod song stuck on repeat. She had sensed THEM before. Why not this time?

As hours stretched thin, Stone's mind drifted to places he didn't want it to go: his past, the faces of colleagues now dust, the future of mankind — or the total annihilation of it. After a thousand years, what waited for them on Earth? Civilization? Or nothing but the silence of ruins? He thought of the Romans, their marble temples now broken teeth in the ground. Was he, too, only a ghost of a dead empire?

Curiously, he couldn't see the aliens themselves. Nothing stirred. No movement. The ship lingered, its presence oppressive, yet it made no approach. Were they irrelevant? Beneath notice?

The ship itself defied comprehension. It loomed like a zeppelin over New York City, only magnified a hundredfold. Its surface wasn't smooth but fractured into planes and ribs, some like the black geometry of the Borg, others curving with organic struts that recalled bones or the carved hull of a cathedral. Vast windows glittered faintly across one flank, and in them—
Stone froze.
Silhouettes.
Shapes like people standing in rows, motionless, watching. Or maybe only shadows. He couldn't tell. The scale made his eyes ache, but the impression of human forms behind alien glass crawled under his skin.

After what seemed like an eternity, but was really only a few hours, the ship stirred. Its bulk shifted, rising. For a heartbeat, everyone thought it was descending toward them, ready to attach, breach, invade. Logan's hand tightened around Stone's without her realizing it.

But the ship didn't come. It rose higher, blotting out the stars as it ascended. Then, as suddenly as it had appeared, it drifted away, shrinking against the black sky until it vanished altogether.

"It's gone," Logan whispered, breaking the silence like glass.

Stone's jaw was locked tight. He turned toward the console, toward the empty air where Cortana's voice should have been. "Now it's time for some answers. Cortana?" he said with an edge in his voice.

Silence.

Chapter 20

Over There

"Cortana?" Stone said aloud. His voice felt too loud, as though the walls might carry it away to ears he didn't want hearing.

Silence.

Then—

—Yes, David.
The voice slid into their heads, colder than before.
—I know what you're thinking. I didn't know They would arrive. Their travel… it is different technology. I count the days They come and go, and it averages twenty-one. But They are not always precise.

Natasha's hands clenched white around her knees.
"What is over there—where they landed?"

—Another part of their base. It is joined to the moon's original port.

Alman blinked hard. "Port? You mean… a way off the moon?"

—If it still functions… yes.

McCarty leaned forward, scowling.
"Don't you know? You said you can be reached anywhere in this base. Isn't that part of it too?"

—No.
Cortana's answer came sharp, clipped.
—That section was cut off long ago. It is… a blind spot. To me. As are other places. Places They still keep for themselves.

McCarty latched onto her final thought.
"Wait… what?!" he blurted out.

Stone's pulse thudded in his ears.
"Take us there. Now."

—With pleasure, Cortana answered, her tone unnervingly bright.

They filed into the massive ATV, the spacious cockpit swallowing them up. Straps clicked. Metal groaned. Behind them, the bulkhead door sealed with a hiss, locking them in.

On the screen, Cortana's map expanded—an impossible bird's-eye mosaic of the moon. Alien structures glittered across the surface, neat as a hive. Some pulsed faintly, like they were breathing.

Warning lights washed the hangar red. Machinery woke with a grinding protest. The massive doors cracked open and the void spilled in, swallowing sound. For an instant, the pressure equalized with a scream of escaping air—like the base itself didn't want to let them go.

The rover shuddered forward. Its heavy treads crunched over

the threshold, biting into regolith. Beyond, Earth's ruined marble stared down at them, cracked and bruised against black infinity.

Stone leaned toward the viewport, his chest tight. Ahead, the horizon sharpened into unnatural geometry: the alien structure where the ship had docked. A sliver of it caught the light, metallic and wrong.

Nobody spoke. The rover bounced across cratered ground, each jolt hammering tension deeper into their bodies.

Finally, Stone risked voicing the thought all of them were swallowing.
lowing.
"What if they left one behind?"

No answer came—not from Cortana, not from the others. Only the quiet rasp of McCarty's breath and Natasha's pulse hammering in her throat.

Then Alman whispered, barely audible:
"Or someone."

The words hung there. Humans? Survivors? Prisoners? Something worse wearing human skin?

No one dared continue the thought.

Cortana remained silent.

Chapter 21

The Port

Cortana slowed the rover to a crawl. Her voice thinned, echoing as if already far away.

—I cannot stay with you inside the Port unless you remain within the rover. Beyond its walls, my presence fades. And remember—this base is old. Not every corridor will be safe. Some may no longer hold pressure at all. If you can please connect my charging cable to the port in the hangar, that will help us keep the rover charged and going.

The warning lingered as the structure loomed ahead.

The Port was massive, unmistakably human in design—straight lines, ribbed supports, the kind of engineering they'd all trained their eyes to recognize. It resembled the base segment attached to where they had awakened, but on a scale several times greater. A command hub dominated the center, and from it stretched long arms leading to the landing pads like gates at an airport. Upon nearly every pad stood a rocket, each one weathered by time yet still proud, relics of a forgotten future.

Stone stared, throat tight. "This was ours," he said softly.

Natasha corrected him. "Was."

The rover hissed to a stop at the outer lock. As they stepped across, Cortana's voice faded completely, leaving only silence.

Natasha investigated the outside of the rover, found the cable, and plugged it in as Cortana had asked. Some lights indicated an active connection.

Inside, the Port swallowed them whole. Mission control spread wide before them, rows of consoles facing darkened glass that looked out over the pads. The chairs stood empty, the stillness suffocating, as though the crew had simply vanished mid-shift.

From this central hub, arms radiated outward. Most ended in the launch bays. Only one veered into something different: a corridor where human angles connected into alien curves.

Alman pointed. "That's the addition. That's where the ship docked."

The air seemed heavier as they stepped into through the airlock into that section. The walls lost their bolts and seams, becoming smooth, flowing, almost organic. Yet the layout was disturbingly familiar: rows of compartments built into the bulkhead, each marked in sequence.

Alman stopped, crouching to trace the glyphs with his finger. "0016… 0017…"
He froze. "0001."

The others gathered, the silence thick with dread.

McCarty tried to laugh but couldn't quite manage it. "You're not actually thinking—"

Stone's hand moved before reason caught him. The drawer sighed open.

A pale light spilled across their faces. Inside, something was forming—half-flesh, half-gel, slowly rising as though grown from liquid crystal. Shoulders. The ridge of a jaw. Fingers not yet separated. A face blurred but unmistakably familiar.

Stone staggered back, his chest heaving.

Natasha whispered, "It's you."

McCarty swore violently and turned away.

Alman's voice was flat, stripped of comfort. "This isn't a morgue. It's a factory. Their structures aren't for mining or inhabiting. This is a nursery. They've been growing us... waiting for harvest."

The unfinished face in the drawer glistened under the sterile light, eyes sealed, mouth not yet formed.

Stone felt the room tilt around him. His voice cracked, a whisper torn from the hollow of his chest.

"If that's me... then who the hell am I?"

No one answered. The unfinished face in the drawer glistened, still knitting itself together, silent and blind.

Stone pressed his palm against the button of the cold bulkhead, the drawer returned, his breath ragged. "And how was I even awake before this? Who released me? Who decided I should walk while the rest stayed locked away?"

The question lingered like static, unanswered, until the only sound was the steady hum of the alien machinery—patient, implacable, waiting.

Chapter 22

Mummies

Mission Control lay in silence, the consoles coated in gray, their lights long gone dim. The air was heavy with dust and the faint tang of oxidized metal, like the breath of a tomb. They sat for a long time, the truth pressing down on them: they were cattle. But for what end? If the aliens could engineer and harvest humanity, why not do so on their own world? Why choose this place, this base, this moon?

They split up. McCarty and Natasha stayed behind at the port, prying into the dormant launch ships and the consoles still clinging to life. Stone, Alman, and Logan pushed deeper into the research wing, where the doors opened reluctantly, releasing stale, trapped air.

The research side of the base was more complete, untouched, almost preserved. Corridors stretched into darkness, laboratories lined with sealed cabinets, living quarters left as if the occupants had only just stepped out. A ghost of human effort, waiting.

McCarty muttered as he tapped uselessly at a console in Mission Control. Then, with a flicker, a screen sputtered to life. McCarty tapped around intuitively until he settled on a station log and opened a file.

Natasha leaned close as an image sharpened: a man's face, pale and hollow-eyed, his voice breaking with exhaustion.

"This is Dr. Jones, Terran Research, December 2341. This may be my last entry. Nearly everyone that was stationed here has died, or tried their luck back on Earth. Earth is returning, but still hostile, filled with creatures from some horror film. The aliens have created some human abominations here on the moon. We tried to fix one—God, we tried—but the DNA isn't ours anymore. There's a failsafe built into it. If the bodies aren't harvested by them, the sequence collapses. They made us into stock."

He coughed, spattering blood, his voice dropping.

"Seed banks… There were two. Arctic—lost, I think. But New Mexico… maybe. If you can find her, maybe there's hope."

His gaze darted aside, his voice lowering to a whisper.

"And if you're new here, just a warning, don't trust Cortana. She's not what you think."

The screen blinked to black. Natasha stared at her reflection in the glass, her lips pressed tight. McCarty swallowed and shut the console down.

Natasha, "There's more to her than what she is sharing. I think she's far more advanced that we can understand, and she knows we wouldn't be able to imagine it."

McCarty, "I don't trust her."

They shared a concerned glance and left Mission Control and made their way back toward the rover.

Meanwhile, in the bioscience wing, Stone, Alman, and Logan passed a window looking into a chamber sealed behind an old airlock.

Rows of bodies lay inside, each arranged deliberately, preserved by vacuum into mummies of skin and bone. Their presence was orderly, intentional, as if the chamber had been designed for this very stillness.

Alistar whispered, "Should we enter?"

Alman shook his head. "No. They're mummified. Could be a thousand years old. Expose them to air and they'll disintegrate."

Logan frowned. "But why mummify a group of researchers?"

Stone's voice was low, speculative. "Preserve the DNA?"

In the next room — cleanroom clean, lined with electronic diagnostic tools — they found her.

A woman's body stood behind a transparent stasis wall. Tall, slender, flawless, clad in a midnight-blue bodysuit etched with a faint hexagonal weave that shimmered when the light caught it. Her face was serene, beautiful, almost unreal — sculpted from an ideal. Eyes closed. Waiting. Preserved in perfect stillness, unaging.

The three entered slowly, approaching the sleeping woman.

On her suit, above the heart, was a mission-style name patch, refined like those worn by Apollo astronauts. It read, simply:

CORTANA.

They froze.

Logan's voice was barely audible. "She's been here all this time. Locked away."

Alman leaned closer, eyes narrowing. "No… look. Here, at her sides. Interface ports. She's not flesh. She's a construct. An android. But she looks human—perfectly."

Stone said nothing. His eyes stayed on the figure, and for the first time, the voice that had guided them felt less like salvation and more like a question.

Back at the port, Natasha and McCarty rejoined the rover. The cabin lights glowed faintly as Cortana's voice met them.

"Cortana, what more can you tell us about Bionaut?" McCarty asked.

Her tone was steady, familiar. She repeated what they had heard before: the harvesting, the cloning, the cycles of creation and collapse. It was the same story they had been told.

And then, after a long pause, she added, her voice quieter:

"But there is more. Much more, it was well documented."

The words hung heavy in the cabin, the promise of revelations that would unravel everything.

Chapter 23

The Fracture

The launch was a spectacle. Cameras swiveled skyward, com-
mentators filled dead air with nervous chatter, and Stone—polished, grinning, wired with adrenaline—was everywhere.

"Why only a thousand?" reporters pressed him in the hours before ignition.

His answer was effortless, rehearsed.
"We're focused on one thousand. To do it right. Once we suc-
ceed, we'll expand. Everyone will have their chance."

It was the kind of line that played well on cable news and in
glossy magazines. He knew it. He loved it. The spotlight was
his oxygen.

But a week later, a whisper broke the surface. On a late-night
segment buried behind political noise, a young employee
appeared on screen. Nervous, unsmiling. She didn't give her
name—only her blurred out face and her story.

She claimed Stone had sold far more than a thousand spots. Tens of thousands. Maybe more. Reporters scrambled, cross-referencing blog posts and family Facebook updates. Everyone seemed to "have a spot," but no one could prove who actually launched. The truth was locked inside Stone's company.

The woman's reason for breaking rank was personal. Her brother, twenty-nine, terminal cancer, had begged for inclusion. She had pleaded with Stone herself. He promised it was taken care of, that her brother's legacy was secured.

Weeks later, walking through the corporate hangar, she discovered a locked storage room. Inside, rows of titanium cryo-capsules stacked like warehouse inventory. She scanned the labels. And there it was—her brother's name, gathering dust. His launch never happened.

After the broadcast, the revelation spread fast. More families came forward. All of them had been reassured. All of them were told they had been chosen. No one could prove who actually made it on the rocket. Six months out, the mystery remained.

By then, the scientists had moved in. Aerospace engineers, geneticists, molecular biologists. They called press conferences, published papers, tweeted threads. Piece by piece, they dismantled Stone's science. "Nonsense," one geneticist said flatly. "Marketing slop, not a technology."

The news cycle cut into him, "Stone's fake launch scheme exposed."

That's when the anger turned organized. A Texas oil baron, aging but flush with money and fury, announced he was filing a class action lawsuit. "Fraud on a scale this country hasn't seen in decades," he told reporters. He hired the best lawyers in Houston and Dallas, and soon thousands signed on. Nearly everyone who bought in joined the case.

Nearly everyone.

Not Amber. Not the handful who knew Stone before the company, back when he was just a broken athlete trying to find purpose. They stayed silent. Out of loyalty, out of love, or perhaps not to distinguish their own hopes and dreams.

The fracture lines had opened. And the weight of it was bearing down on Stone.

Late one night, when the newsroom feeds had thinned to a handful of ticker headlines, like "Bio-NOTS failed launch racket", Stone sat alone in the company's top-floor conference room watching the lawsuit grow into a thing that could swallow him. The building had emptied hours before; security doors sealed, fluorescent lights dimmed. On a muted monitor, pundits argued about intent and jurisdiction as if their opinions could be considered the final verdict.

He looked at his laptop, a long list of names, from one to a thousand. The title read "Final Manifest". He saved the file, sent it through Signal to some other account, then…he deleted it. He paused and then wiped his drive clean and reinstalled the operating system fresh. No files, no emails, no nothing. He then admin logged into his email server and deleted any and all emails he had ever sent from Bionaut. Finally, he went to the LTO backups and erased all of the backup files. There would be no trace.

He left the conference room and walked the long industrial corridor toward the storage wing. The company smelled of ozone and cleansers. Machines hummed in standby. In the dim emergency lights the assembly floor felt like a stage cleared after the show.

His hand clicked the storeroom door open. Inside were rows of small capsules—titanium, neat, clinical. They were no larger than a large supplement capsule, each one stamped cleanly with a person's name and date of birth. Up close they looked absurdly intimate: a lifetime reduced to a tiny metal oblong.

He stood there for a long minute and imagined matches, hammers, microscopes. Burn the evidence. Wipe the ledger. Make it look like a filing error. Make it look like nothing had ever happened here. It would be simple, stupid, and final. If the law could not find the evidence, the trial would be theater and he could walk away.

He could not bring himself to destroy them.

But he also could not leave them where they would be used to tear him apart in full public view.

So he did the only thing his contradictory conscience would allow. He gathered them.

One by one he slipped the capsules into a heavy canvas bag, the metal cold against his palms. He did not check names except by the light of habit—two he paused over and set aside for a breath, then into the bag with the others. When the bag was full it had the weight of consequence.

He spent the next four hours sanitizing the room until it looked like a fresh storage space in a newly leased facility: wiped shelving, vacuumed corners, resealed labels with blank tape, rearranged boxes to cover the area where the cases had been. He scrubbed fingerprints off the handles; he ran the closet lights on a timer to simulate normal use; he reset the RFID logs he could access through admin consoles until they told a story of disuse instead of hiding.

When the subpoena came—and it would come—when investigators and lawyers and cameras came combing, they would find a clean room and no inventory. They would find an empty shelf where a pile of unlaunched Bionauts had sat. They would find nothing tying Stone to the people who had been promised a future.

He zipped the canvas bag and slung it over his shoulder. The bag was warm from his hands. He walked out of the storeroom past the dark rows of equipment, past the sleeping offices, and into the cold night. He did not know yet where he would take them, what he would do with what he held. He only knew he could not leave them to be used against him.

Outside, the city smelled like rain. Stone walked away into the glare of the streetlights and the hush of a world that, for the moment, was still waiting to learn the truth.

Chapter 24

The Truth

McCarty and Ivanchenko sat in the rover long after the console went dark.
The voice of the dying man still echoed in the silence.

Don't trust Cortana. She's not what you think.

He hadn't said who he was, only "Dr. Jones, Terran Research." Just another ghost of the old world—one more voice trapped in the machinery of the base.

Natasha finally broke the silence. "He was here. You heard the background—same walls, same air vents. That recording was made here."
McCarty nodded. "Yeah. And he was bleeding out when he said it. Whatever happened, it wasn't quick."

They didn't speak her name again. Not out loud.

When Stone, Alman, and Logan returned, their expressions

told the story before they spoke.

Stone's face was pale beneath the dust. "We found something," he said quietly.

McCarty stood. "What?"

"A body," Alman said. "Female. Standing upright behind a transparent wall."

Logan's voice was thin. "She looked human. Perfect. But she isn't. Interface ports under the ribs, synthetic fibers under the skin."

Natasha's stomach turned. "Cortana."

Stone gave a small nod. "That name's on her suit. She's been here, sealed up, maybe for centuries, but why?"

McCarty stood. "Well, we found something, too." McCarty shared the contents of the video message him and Natasha had seen.

McCarty swallowed hard. "That message—whoever Jones was—he was warning us about her."

Stone frowned. "You think she killed them?"

"I don't know," McCarty said. "But he sure didn't sound like someone who trusted her. Said the clones were collapsing, the DNA wasn't human anymore, and that she—whatever she is—couldn't be trusted."

Silence stretched, thick and uneasy.

Stone rubbed his hands over his face. "Maybe he was right. Maybe she's been listening this whole time. We know she has the ability."

Logan crossed her arms. "If she's awake enough to talk, she's awake enough to hear."

Stone nodded slowly. "Then from now on we assume the walls have ears."
He turned to Natasha. "Those ships—can they still fly?"

"They respond and appear intact." she said. "Whether they'll reach Earth? No guarantee."

Stone gave a dark half-smile. "If we don't, maybe one of our clones will."

No one laughed.

He looked back toward the corridor that led to the research wing. "Perhaps she's quarantined in that section for a reason. Nobody goes near it alone. Nobody calls her name. If she's still active, we don't want her knowing we know."

He paused at the doorway, voice dropping to a whisper.

"Whatever's behind that glass—it's not our friend."

Chapter 25

Earthfall

The ship hummed to life on its own, like it had been waiting for them.

Natasha stood at the primary console, hands hovering over controls that responded before she touched them.
"I didn't activate it," she said. "Autopilot just… engaged."

Stone leaned forward. "Destination?"

"Earth," she said. "Looks like it was pre-programmed."

Alman frowned. "By who?"

No one answered.

The docking clamps released with a metallic sigh. A deep vibration rolled through the floor as the craft lifted from the lunar pad—slow, deliberate, like an old animal waking from hibernation.

Outside, the gray landscape fell away. The moon's horizon shimmered, then disappeared into black.

McCarty watched from the rear viewport. "Hard to believe this place kept us alive."

Stone didn't look back. "Harder to believe we'll survive what's next."

Minutes later, the Earth filled the forward window — enormous, shrouded, almost bruised-looking. Brown cloud belts streaked the continents; the ocean was darker, with wide, silver sheens where light reflected off something viscous, not water.

Natasha frowned at her screen. "Atmospheric readings are inconsistent. Temperature gradients all over the place. No sign of orbital traffic."

Logan peered closer. "What's that light—southern hemisphere?"

"Not sunlight," Natasha said. "Thermal bloom. Probably volcanic."

A jolt rocked the ship.
The lights dimmed, then flickered back on.
McCarty checked a secondary panel. "One of the stabilizers just cycled off."

"Will we make it?" Stone asked.

"I don't know," McCarty said. "It's advanced human tech. I don't even understand half the readouts."

The ship began to vibrate harder. Warning glyphs scrolled across the display—red symbols none of them could read.

"Altitude control's automated," Natasha said. "We can't override. We just… trust it."

Another shudder — a deep metallic groan from the hull. The cabin lighting strobed, briefly plunging them into darkness.

Then, as quickly as it began, the vibration smoothed out. Outside, the planet grew massive — blue edges burning bright against space.

"Re-entry burn commencing," the console announced in a calm, synthetic voice. None of them recognized it.

McCarty swallowed. "Who the hell was that?"

Natasha looked uneasy. "Not me."

The ship hit the upper atmosphere.
A sheath of plasma flared across the windows, white-hot light rippling over the hull. The noise was deafening — a roar that filled their bones.

They held on. No one spoke.
The entire cabin shuddered as the heat grew, the ship compressing under forces they could barely comprehend.

Then — silence.

The fire faded. Clouds streaked by below.
Through the smoke, they saw a coastline — not the blue-green of old Earth, but ash-gray, carved by strange, swollen seas.

Natasha squinted at her screen. "Autopilot's shifting course—inland. Toward a beacon."

Stone moved beside her. "New Mexico?"

She nodded. "That's what the map says. If you can call it a map anymore."

The craft descended through layers of haze. Cities appeared — not alive, but skeletal.
Towers half-submerged. Rusted domes and twisted metal protruding from the water.
Nothing moved below them but wind and waves.

"Are we sure this is home?" Logan whispered.

McCarty answered softly. "It used to be."

A burst of static hit the comm system.
A faint rhythmic signal cut through — one-two-three, pause, one-two-three.

Natasha turned. "That's the beacon. It's real."

Stone nodded once. "Then we follow it."

The ship banked gently and began its final descent, disappearing through the cloud cover toward the ruins below.

Behind them, far across the void, the lunar base flickered once—
a soft pulse in the bioscience wing, like a heartbeat returning.

Chapter 26

The Beacon

The descent craft jolted hard as it cut through the lower atmosphere.
Dust and static arced across the forward canopy. Autopilot
hissed through corrections, metal groaning under reentry heat.
The Earth below was gray and broken — veins of salt and ash,
clouds the color of old bruises.

Stone gripped the armrest.
"Anyone seeing a city down there?"

No one answered. There were no cities.

When they finally touched down, the ship settled into silence.
Dust swirled around them, thicker than fog, coating everything
in a pale film. For a long moment, no one spoke.

Then Natasha unstrapped, stood, and crossed to a panel at the
rear of the cabin. She brushed away a layer of dust revealing a
recessed handle, then hesitated.

"Before we go outside," she said, "we might want to look at this."

She grabbed a handle to open a locker. It briefly read turned red, "Biosignature not recognized, then green, "Biosignature confirmed." McCarty winked to Natasha. She pulled the panel open. Inside were three matte-black rifles clipped to a rack — their surfaces faintly luminescent, powered by some internal core.

Stone frowned. "Weapons?"

"I think so," Natasha said. "They were in the manifest… under 'EM Containment.' No idea why."

Logan stepped closer, eyes lighting up. "Pulse rifles." She ran a finger along the coil chamber. "Short-range electromagnetic discharge. Saw something like it in a sci-fi film."

McCarty raised a skeptical eyebrow. "You really think they'll work after a thousand years?"

"Only one way to find out," Stone said.

Logan slung one over her shoulder. Stone took the next. Natasha hesitated before taking the third, weighing it uncertainly.

Alman raised his hands. "I don't shoot. I calculate."

McCarty smirked. "Same. But I've seen *Aliens*. I know how this turns out without a weapon."

Stone gave a tight half-smile. "Then stay close."

He hit the hatch release. The outer seal disengaged with a hiss that echoed through the cabin like a sigh.

The ramp lowered into a world that should have been dead —

but wasn't.
Wind moved in slow, heavy gusts across a field of silted plains. Half-buried antennae and the ribs of old structures jutted from the sand like fossils. The air shimmered with static. Somewhere beyond the horizon, a beacon pulsed in short bursts — rhythmic, mechanical, and human.

— . .⎯ ⎯.⎯. ⎯⎯⎯ ⎯... . .⎯ ⎯.⎯. ⎯⎯⎯ ⎯... . .⎯ ⎯.⎯. ⎯⎯⎯ —

It was the first sound of life they'd heard since leaving the moon.

Chapter 27

The Serengeti of New Mexico

At the end of the ramp was a New Mexico no one remembered — a vast, shimmering plain of tall grass and amber light, broken in the far distance by a thick, dark-green band of jungle. Not a forest. A wall. A living, humid engine of oxygen and shadow.

"Well… not the New Mexico we were expecting."

The air shimmered with heat. Strange winged things drifted between the plains and jungle line — not birds, not quite anything.

McCarty whistled. "Christ. This looks like Jurassic Park met *Lawrence of Arabia*."

They stepped outside, one by one, pulse rifles slung, boots sinking into soft loam. The air was wet, heavy with pollen and ozone. Above them, a leathery silhouette with translucent wings caught the sun and vanished into the green.

Stone studied the horizon, unsettled. "How the hell does this exist here? After a thousand years?"

Alman crouched to examine the earth. It was rich, almost over-ripe. "The world doesn't die easy," he murmured. "It adapts. The spike hits must have shuffled the plates."

Then came a sound — deep, guttural, like a horse clearing its throat.

A creature stood a hundred meters away, half in shadow: long-bodied, reptilian, copper-skinned. Its forelimbs ended in hooves, flank shimmering like armor.

Logan whispered, "What is that?"

"Something that's been waiting for lunch," McCarty muttered. "And we're about to get eaten."

The creature studied them, then trotted away, more curious than afraid.

Natasha raised her scanner. "I'm getting faint EM pulses that way," she said, pointing past the plains toward the jungle wall. "Could be the bunker beacon bouncing around the terrain."

Stone shaded his eyes. "Then that's our path — across this plain, through that jungle, and whatever's beyond."

McCarty spat. "Fantastic. Ten kilometers of things with scales, claws, and teeth."

"Stay tight," Logan said. "Whatever's alive out here, it's watch-ing us."

Alman nodded. "Watching," he said softly, "but not attacking. Yet."

They started walking — five figures crossing a prehistoric plain reborn. Above them, glass-winged pterosaurs tilted on the thermals. The grass rippled around their knees with unseen life.

And ahead, somewhere deep past the jungle's green wall, a faint, rhythmic pulse echoed — patient, metallic.

A signal that had never stopped waiting.

Chapter 28

The Jungle Crossing

The jungle swallowed them whole.

One step they were in golden light; the next they were under a cathedral of vines and steam. Leaves the size of shields dripped condensation. Bioluminescent insects clicked in brief flashes. Every breath felt thick enough to chew.

"Ten kilometers," Natasha said, studying the jittering arrow on the scavenged beacon. "Signal's coming from beyond this, not inside it."

McCarty groaned. "Great. We get the fun part first."

The first hour was only noise — dripping water, screeching life, distant crashes of something large moving parallel to their route.

Then came the vines.

Glossy, black, pulsing with faint internal light. Stone sliced one free with a flick of his blade.

It recoiled.

"That's alive," Logan said sharply. "Don't touch them."

The vines reacted to heat. They had to slow down, move carefully, weaving between them like threads in a loom.

After another klick, the ground softened. Mud pits disguised beneath leaf litter sucked at their feet. Stone nearly vanished waist-deep before Logan hauled him out. McCarty fell next, cursing until Alman used a broken branch as a lever.

"They're traps," Natasha said. "Carnivorous root systems waiting for anything with mass."

"Fantastic," McCarty said, wiping mud from his face. "Ten kilometers of sentient spaghetti."

They pressed on.

Halfway through the jungle, a new sound followed them — low-bodied shapes pacing them in the shadows, spines glinting like wet armor when shafts of light pierced the canopy.

"Same things from the plains?" Logan whispered.

"No," Alman said, voice small. "These are bigger."

A howl rolled through the underbrush — deep, resonant, furnace-like.

"Move," Stone said.

The path narrowed. The creatures herded them, pushing them toward a thin strip of solid clearing — vines swayed, ground quivered. They had no choice but to break into a sprint.

A blur shot from the left — a feline-like, spotted creature with translucent jaws snapped inches from Logan's shoulder.

She stumbled—

—and her body blurred. The air rippled around her.

"Logan?" Stone gasped.

"Don't move!" she hissed. "Just think it. Think hide!"

Stone closed his eyes, focused—

—and the world folded. His hands vanished.

"Everyone! Do it now!"

Natasha vanished first, then McCarty. The beasts skidded to a halt, confused, sniffing the space where bodies should've been.

All except Alman.

"I—I can't," he stammered, shaking. Solid. Visible.

One beast fixed on him and lunged.

"Alman!" Logan's unseen voice snapped. "Focus!"

He vanished an instant before impact and ducked.

The creature crashed into a root cluster, snarling, then padded away.

They remained still until the pack gave up.

Then Logan exposed only her fist. "Follow my hand."

One by one, faint shimmering silhouettes drifted after her until they reached the far end of the jungle — a wall of green parting into blinding light.

And ahead…

An open scree field leading to a small rise of jagged mountains.

Ash-colored grass. Arid wind, the outer skin of the bunker's perimeter.

Stone exhaled. "Everyone okay?"

A shimmer beside him resolved into Logan. "Yeah. But I don't want to test that twice."

McCarty coughed out a nervous laugh. "I think a polar bear was more apex."

Stone ignored him, staring at the horizon.

"No," he murmured. "Not anymore. But we might still be the clever ones."

Behind them, something hulking with a disturbingly human face watched from the jungle's edge — a predator dissecting the team's escape.

They pushed through the last stretch of jungle, the canopy thinning until sunlight began to stab through the leaves. Then the trees broke—and the mountains hit them like a wall. A jagged line of stone rose straight out of the plain, sharp and pale, the kind of climb you feel just by looking at it. The beacon's pulse came from somewhere beyond those ridges. Stone exhaled, already knowing what came next.

"Fantastic," McCarty said. "Ten klicks of murder-jungle and

now this. Perfect."

Logan tightened her pack. "Better than staying here."

She glanced behind them at the dark green tangle, where something large moved but never showed itself.

No one argued. They stepped out of the jungle and headed for the rock.

Chapter 29

The Perimeter

They crested the final ridge in the late afternoon. A low valley opened before them below—flat, windless, eerily still. The air carried no scent of life. Whatever vegetation grew here was brittle and gray-green, shaped by centuries of radiation and silence.

They made their way down the side of the mountain and greeted the flat surface with relief and gratitude.

At the valley's center stood the beacon's source.

Natasha's handheld tracker pulsed softly in her palm, its faint blue light syncing with each step. "Signal's strong—five hundred meters, maybe less."

The others slowed, scanning the horizon. At first there was nothing. Then, half-buried in the valley floor, a small concrete structure took shape—sloped walls, vent pipes, and an angular entry face dulled to the same color as the earth around it.

"Doesn't look like much," McCarty muttered. "Maybe a weather station."
"No," Stone said. "That's engineered. Reinforced."

From a distance it could've passed for an abandoned utility shed, but the symmetry gave it away—every edge poured with intent, every seam built to withstand the unthinkable.

They approached slowly, camouflaged bodies flickering like heat distortion against the terrain. Only Alman struggled; his shimmer faltered, flashing in and out like a bad hologram.
"Hold it together," Logan warned quietly. "You're glowing again."
"I'm trying," he hissed.

A deep *whump* echoed across the plain. Then another.
They dropped instinctively.

Out in the open, something large tore from the brush—a reptilian beast, horse-sized, mottled skin glinting with scale and oil. It let out a rasping screech and charged straight for the structure.

Natasha turned to engage it, lowering her pulse rifle with ease.

Suddenly a turret embedded near the entry slope came alive. Its triple barrels spun up with a piercing hum.
One pulse—pure white plasma—slammed into the creature, tearing through it mid-stride. The sound of its death rolled out across the plain and vanished into the wind.

Silence.

"Jesus," McCarty whispered. "Still operational."
Natasha crouched, eyes scanning, seeing other turrets around the perimeter. "Only one. The rest are long gone."

The others followed her gaze. Scattered through the field were half-buried sentry guns, their frames rusted through, optics shattered, chassis overgrown with *vines.*

At first they looked ordinary—dry, tangled growth clinging to steel—but as the team drew closer, the vines shimmered. Thin metallic filaments ran through each tendril, pulsing with faint green light, as if sap and current shared the same veins.

McCarty reached out and tapped one with his rifle barrel. The vine recoiled, smaller filaments snapping back into cracks in the wall.
"Jesus," he said again. "It's breathing."

Stone crouched beside a strand, watching tiny bioluminescent motes drift within its translucent skin. The vine disappeared into a vent grille near the main blast door—feeding power, or something stranger, into the bunker's heart.
"Looks like the whole structure's wired into the root system," Alman said.
"Or the other way around," Stone murmured.

The active turret whined softly, then powered down.
"Why didn't it fire at us?" Alman asked, voice tight.
Stone's eyes narrowed. "It recognizes us. Maybe our DNA, heat signatures—something human."
"Or close enough," Logan said with a twisted smile.

Alman's shimmer steadied. For the first time, they were fully invisible.
"Move," Stone said quietly. "Before it rethinks the rules."

They crossed the final stretch in silence. Up close, the bunker was smaller than expected but far denser—its concrete thick with rebar veins, the entry slab rising from the soil like a tomb-stone. The air was cold and metallic here, tinged with ozone from the turret's recent discharge and the faint electric scent of the living vines.

A faint wind moaned through a rusted vent pipe. Beneath it, a heavy access door sat flush with the wall, edges blackened by age.

Stone stepped forward, brushing a hand across its surface. Dust came off in thick gray streaks. Beneath it, the suggestion of letters—subtle, recessed.
He wiped again, harder. The grit fell away, revealing lines of text cast directly into the concrete, the letters sunk deep like ancient inscriptions.

UNITED STATES STRATEGIC RESEARCH COMMAND
Below it: **BIO-DEFENSE DIVISION.**

"They built this to last," Stone murmured, tracing a fingertip along the groove of the "S." "Not for a decade—for a millennium. Whoever made this wanted to be remembered."
Logan ran her hand beside his. "Looks like they got their wish."

Stone's palm lingered on the cold concrete, feeling the weight of the centuries in its touch.
He stepped back, studying the sealed access door with its large steel handle. "The perimeter's still guarding whatever's inside," he said quietly.
Stone nodded once. "Let's find out if it remembers us."

He exhaled and let his shoulders relax. The shimmer around him flickered, then dissolved. His normal clothing—dusty, torn, human—returned in full view.
Logan noticed first, then smiled faintly. "Guess the show's over."

One by one, the others followed suit, their camouflage fading away until they all stood visible again, framed against the bunker's pale concrete and the slow-pulsing light of the biomech vines.

For the first time since they'd landed, they looked like people again—tired, wary, but unmistakably human.
And together, no longer ghosts, they approached the door—
the last of their kind, standing at the edge of a forgotten world beneath the earth.

Chapter 30

The Perimeter

The steel handle was cold to the touch, yet alive.
When Stone's fingers wrapped around it, a faint vibration
pulsed through the metal—like something deep inside the
mechanism was listening. Then came a click, heavy and ancient, followed by a low groan of machinery that sounded like
it hadn't moved in centuries.

Massive gears engaged beyond the door. The sound reverber-
ated through the concrete, deep and resonant, as if the whole
structure were stirring awake. Then, suddenly, silence—followed by a soft mechanical sigh. The handle turned without
resistance. The door, thick as a vault, opened effortlessly, gliding
inward as though on air.

A breath of clean, temperate air drifted out.

Inside was a circular stairwell—poured concrete walls so
smooth they seemed molded in a single piece. Narrow slits of

light ran continuously along the ceiling, cool and even, with no visible source. The air smelled faintly sterile, like rainwater and stone.

Alman stepped in behind Stone, took a slow breath, and said, "Feels… comfortable. Like someone's been running the heat for us."

"Finally something on this planet that isn't trying to kill us," McCarty muttered.

Stone nodded, stepping onto the first stair. The concrete gave no sound beneath his boots.
The others followed—Logan, Natasha, Alman, and McCarty—each of them casting quick looks over their shoulders as they descended the spiral.

The moment the last foot left the threshold, the door above them silently closed shut.
A single, resonant clang shook the stairwell, followed by the unmistakable sound of bolts driving home. The light flickered once, then steadied.

McCarty tilted his head back. "Guess we're not goin' back up that way."

"Forward's always been the plan," Stone said. His tone was calm, but his jaw was tight.

For several minutes, the only sounds were their footsteps and breathing. The descent curved steadily downward—no branching corridors, no markings, no dust. Everything looked new. Too new.

Then Logan slowed, frowning.
"Hold on," she said quietly.

The wall beside her wasn't perfectly smooth anymore. A faint, organic pattern—like veins beneath translucent skin—ran through the concrete, twisting gently in the light. She brushed her fingers across it. The texture was cool, slightly pliant, and pulsed once beneath her touch.

Alman recoiled. "What the hell was that?"

Natasha leaned closer, squinting. "Not roots. Some kind of integrated lattice. Maybe bio-reactive reinforcement?"

The faint veins receded almost instantly, the wall returning to its flawless gray. The group stared at it for a moment longer, unsure whether it had truly moved.

McCarty exhaled. "Concrete shouldn't *breathe*."

Stone glanced upward at the seamless ceiling. "Maybe nothing here should."

They pressed on, the sound of their steps more cautious now.

Finally, Logan broke the silence again.
"That camouflage trick back there…" she said, her voice echoing faintly in the circular shaft. "How did we do that? I didn't even think—it just happened."

"Adrenaline," Natasha said. "Maybe instinct triggered something in our skin, like an Octopus."

"Then why didn't Alman's work until the last second?" McCarty added.

Alman glanced back. "Because I'm human enough to panic first."

The group laughed softly, tension bleeding off for a moment. But even as they did, the lights overhead shifted—almost imperceptibly—from white to a faint amber tone.

Stone stopped. "Hold up."

A low, harmonic hum filled the stairwell, as if the walls themselves were vibrating. Then the voice came—flat, mechanical, but unmistakably human and clear.

"Welcome to the Bio-Defense Research Facility. Identification in progress."

The words rolled down the stairwell like a wave—clear, English, and impossibly calm after what must have been millennia.

McCarty whispered, "English. Did it just say *welcome?*"

Before anyone could answer, a series of lines appeared on the walls—narrow slits opening with precise symmetry. From within each slit emerged a faint, scanning beam of blue light. It swept the stairwell in sections, moving deliberately from one person to the next.

They froze.

The first beam passed over Logan—steady blue. Over McCarty—steady. Over Stone—steady.

Then it reached Alman.
The beam paused. Flickered.
Red.

"Uh, guys…" Alman whispered.

The light pulsed once, then twice, before finally shifting back to blue. A sharp chime sounded—confirmation of something— then the slits sealed seamlessly back into the concrete.

Everyone exhaled at once.

"What the hell was that?" McCarty said.

"Bio-authentication?" Natasha replied. "A security layer. Maybe it's checking who—or *what*—we are."

Stone looked down the stairwell. The lights ahead had turned green, as if giving them permission to continue.
"Then it knows we're human."

Logan met his eyes. "For now."

They resumed the descent, slower this time. Every footstep echoed longer than the one before, as though the space beneath them was widening. The hum of machinery receded, replaced by something subtler—a heartbeat rhythm deep in the foundation.

At twenty-five meters down, the stairs ended in a circular landing. Another door waited below, identical to the first, but this one already stood slightly ajar. A faint draft escaped through the gap—ozone, crisp, fresh, and a little cooler.

McCarty looked around. "Who opened it?"

No one answered.

Stone moved to the door and stared through the narrow slit of light beyond.
"Let's find out," he said.

And with a soft push, Stone and the team stepped through the doorway.

Chapter 31

Serenity

The door opened with a quiet sigh, releasing a faint current of air that smelled like rain after a long drought—clean, cool, and alive.

Beyond it stretched a chamber vast enough to swallow their voices. Glass and steel containers shimmered with soft internal light, and inside them floated human shapes—some complete, others fragmented, like figures half-dreamed. The low hum of machinery resonated beneath it all, steady as a heartbeat.

Stone stepped through first, eyes sweeping the room. "Stay close."

The others followed, their reflections sliding over the polished floor. The stillness pressed in, thick and reverent, as if they'd stepped into a cathedral built for science.

Then movement—a silhouette gliding between the columns.

A woman stepped into view.

She was tall, elegant, and radiantly calm. Her face was human in every way, yet refined beyond nature—features balanced with impossible precision, eyes a soft and living blue, her expression open and kind. There was warmth in her presence, the kind that immediately disarmed fear.

She smiled gently. "How was your journey?"

Her voice was soft, melodic, and sincere—so human it felt like home.

Stone hesitated, caught off guard by the tone. "Long," he said. "And strange."

"I can imagine," she replied. "You've come a very long way."

She stepped closer, her movements fluid, almost musical. "I am *Serenity.*"

Logan whispered, "Is she an android?"

Serenity nodded slightly, unoffended. "Yes. I was created to assist Doctor Sidorov. My purpose is to help, to care for this place, and to welcome anyone who might someday return."

Natasha studied her. "You've been here all this time?"

"Yes," Serenity said softly. "The world outside grew quiet. I kept the systems running, the records safe. I hoped… someday, someone might come back."

Her eyes held a trace of wistfulness that was unmistakably human.

McCarty glanced around the chamber. "What exactly was Sidorov doing here?"

Serenity raised her hand slightly. Around them, faint holograms flickered to life—anatomical forms, rotating DNA helixes, maps of cellular structures merging and dividing in luminous patterns.

"This was a sanctuary," she said. "A place to study what humanity might become. Doctor Sidorov believed the body could be strengthened, the mind expanded, the spirit… preserved. She called it *the Ascension Genome.*"

Alman frowned. "Immortality?"

Serenity's eyes softened. "She preferred to think of it as *continuance.* A life unbound by time, but still capable of compassion."

Natasha asked quietly, "And where is she now?"

Serenity hesitated—an almost human pause. "I haven't seen her in a while."

Stone folded his arms. "Then she's dead. After all this time, how could she not be?"

Serenity welcoming their curiosity, "Come, I'll show you around." As she moved away from the entry area, and towards a metallic corridor.

Chapter 32

Dinner is Served

The corridor widened into a cavernous chamber, half metal, half carved stone. Lights flickered on in sequence, revealing catwalks, suspended cables, and machines older than any of them could date. Serenity stepped into one alcove ahead of them.

As the team took it all in, a door slid open on the far end. A woman stood framed in the light beyond it slim, composed, her movements confident. She looked no older than thirty-five. Her hair was tied loosely at the back, her clothes casual and impossibly anachronistic: faded Levi's 501s and a black baby-doll T-shirt, worn soft with age. Her bare feet made no sound against the warm floor.

"Welcome," she said in a smooth Russian accent. "The travelers from above."

Stone froze. "Dr. Sidorov?"

"The one and only," she said with a warm smile that didn't

quite reach her eyes. "And you, Stone, the man who promised 1000 lives and delivered none…perhaps history misjudged you."

The team exchanged glances, wondering. Serenity, who had re-appeared beside them without sound, bowed her head slightly, as if acknowledging her superior.

Sidorov stepped closer, her heels clicking softly on the floor. "My, my… look at you all. So young. So alive." Her gaze lingered on each of them a moment too long, like she was studying specimens under glass.

Logan shifted her weight. "You're the only one here?"

"For now," Sidorov replied, unfazed. "The others — well, they didn't adapt as well as I had hoped. But enough grim talk! You've traveled far. You must be starving."

She turned, gesturing for them to follow.

They moved through a maze of hallways—clean, humming, impossibly maintained. The air itself seemed alive, vibrating faintly with the pulse of distant generators. Conduits ran through the walls like veins, their faint blue glow suggesting a circulatory system for the entire bunker.

Sidorov led them briskly, her voice echoing softly against the steel and glass. "This facility was designed for one purpose—continuity. It will outlive every surface ruin on Earth."

They passed a transparent door revealing a hydroponic garden glowing with emerald light. Rows of leafy growth floated in nutrient mist, tended by slow, graceful robotic arms. Another android, though appearing less advanced as Serenity. The next chamber revealed something less peaceful—rows of biotanks, each one churning with a cloudy, amber fluid. Within, indistinct forms shifted, half-grown, half-sleeping.

A few corridors later, they reached a vaulted laboratory dominated by a glass cylinder at least twenty feet high. Inside, suspended by cables and fluid, loomed a figure—humanoid but grotesquely enlarged, its musculature rippling like braided steel. Its eyes were sealed, but its chest rose and fell as if it dreamed of waking.

McCarty froze. "Jesus Christ… What the hell is that? A *Resident Evil* Nemesis?"

Sidorov didn't slow. "Just another attempt to help humanity survive."

Her tone was neutral, almost academic—but it carried a chill that silenced them all.

The others exchanged uneasy glances. The monstrous hulk could have torn a man in half; the idea that it was meant to *help* humanity sounded like a cruel joke.

Under his breath, Alman whispered, almost to steady himself, "That's a cave troll. It is. It is."

No one answered.

Moments later they emerged into an intimate, warm dining chamber lined with brushed metal and low, indirect light. A table had been set with glassware, bottles, and steaming platters—the first warmth they'd seen since entering the base.

Sidorov spread her arms with quiet pride.
"You see?" she said. "Civilization still lives."

The table was laid out — real food, steaming bowls of stew, bread, even wine. The aroma hit them hard after days of survival rations.

McCarty stared. "I don't even care if it's poison."

Sidorov laughed, a low melodic sound. "It isn't. I promise."

She lifted a silver lid from the center platter, releasing a wave of rich, savory steam. A roast glistened beneath the light, the skin bronzed and crackling, the scent somewhere between pork and something wilder.

"This," she said with quiet pride, "is *Long Marrowhorn Boar*. A resilient species we keep here. One of my earliest successes."

Alman leaned forward, entranced. "Smells… unreal."

Sidorov carved with precise movements, thin slices falling like silk to each plate. The meat was perfectly marbled, tender, almost too tender.

They ate in silence for a few minutes, the only sound the clink of utensils.

McCarty finally broke the spell. "I don't even know what this is, but if there's a god left, he lives in your kitchen."

Sidorov smiled. "It is… nourishing. You'll feel stronger soon."

Stone nodded appreciatively, chewing slowly. "You're right about that."

Wine flowed easily after that — a deep amber vintage that smelled faintly of honey and ozone. The sharp edges of exhaustion softened; conversation loosened.

McCarty leaned back, flushed. "You realize we just made it from the moon to New Mexico, through hell itself, and now we're drinking wine underground? That's got to be worth a toast."

Stone lifted his glass. "To the impossible."

They clinked glasses. Laughter rippled through the room, weary but genuine.

Natasha's cheeks were pink, her usual precision fading to warmth. "You ever think maybe this is it? Maybe we're the last ones?"

Alman shook his head. "If we are, then maybe we deserve this dinner."

For a moment, the bunker felt human again — voices, warmth, a fragile flicker of the world they'd lost.

Then Logan noticed Sidorov.

The doctor was eating quietly, but something about the rhythm of it caught her eye — too deliberate, too hungry. Sidorov's knife moved faster now, cutting thick pieces, her lips slick with juice, chewing almost greedily. There was a faint sound — a low, wet growl — before she seemed to catch herself.

She looked up, meeting Logan's gaze. For an instant her expression was naked, feral. Then it was gone. Sidorov dabbed her mouth with a napkin and smiled as if nothing had happened.

"Please," she said softly, "enjoy yourselves. You've earned this."

But the room had gone quieter. No one said anything. They just kept eating, slower now, the air heavy with something they couldn't name.

A few minutes later Sidorov rose, voice smooth again.
"The rooms are ready. You'll find the beds soft, the air clean. Rest. Tomorrow you'll see our true work."

She turned and walked away, the echo of her footsteps trailing like the slow padder of a mouse.

When the door closed, Logan whispered, "Tell me you saw that."

Stone's jaw tightened. "I saw."

Far below them, faint through the floor, something moved — mechanical, alive, and waiting.

Chapter 33

The Death Switch

Away from the dining room the lab was silent except for the faint, rhythmic hum of the processors — a mechanical heartbeat that never tired.
Pale light washed across the room, illuminating rows of translucent panels where genetic data floated like suspended galaxies.

Serenity stood before them, motionless.
Four sequences revolved in the air — Stone, Natasha, McCarty, Alman — each rendered as a glowing double helix. She studied them without emotion. They were not people to her. They were variables. Possible templates. Solutions.

The door slid open with a whisper.
Dr. Sidorov entered, the faint shuffle of her boots breaking the quiet. Her expression was drawn, her voice rough with exhaustion. "You've been running these sequences for hours. What are you seeing?"

Serenity didn't look up. "Patterns that shouldn't exist."

A flick of her wrist magnified one strand. A thin crimson filament pulsed within it, woven neatly through the human code like a hidden thread in a tapestry.

Sidorov approached, squinting. "That segment… it's synthetic."

"Yes. Identical in all four genomes." Serenity's tone was even, almost clinical. "Whoever inserted it understood the human nervous system intimately. It's not part of any natural lineage."

"What does it do?"

Serenity rotated the image. The red thread expanded, unfolding into a lattice of control nodes. "It interfaces with the autonomic system — cardiac rhythm, pulmonary flow, vascular tone. It remains dormant until it receives the correct signal."

Sidorov frowned. "Signal?"

"A biochemical or electrical key or catalyst," Serenity replied. "Once activated, it can halt the heart, suppress respiration, or induce neural paralysis. A death command, encoded at birth."

Sidorov exhaled slowly. "To what end?"

Serenity's voice was steady. "Control. One signal, and every cell obeys. It's not an accident — it's architecture. They built obedience into the genome itself."

Sidorov's gaze darkened. "They knew us that well."

"They did," Serenity said. "The alien base wasn't born of ignorance. It was constructed *after* humanity's annihilation. They studied what we were — our defiance, our will to rebel — and they corrected it. They knew freedom would breed resistance so they engineered a species incapable of it."

The air between them felt heavier. The rotating helix cast a faint red glow across Sidorov's face.

She crossed her arms. "When was it done?"

Serenity opened another projection — fragmentary lunar archives, recovered from damaged systems. "After the fall. The alien base came later. They found remnants of the Bionaut program — a single cryo-tray of preserved human DNA — and reconstructed them from that."

Sidorov's expression tightened. "Replication, not resurrection."

"Exactly. The Bionauts we see are derivatives, designed for servitude. They are not survivors of the old mission. They were manufactured long after the original species had perished."

Sidorov's voice turned cold. "Then they aren't human."

Serenity regarded the helix. "Not in the original sense. They were made to resemble us, but their loyalty is hard-coded. They are property."

Silence filled the lab — deep, clinical, suffocating.

Sidorov turned toward the observation window, her reflection fractured by the glass. "Well, I guess that tells us more about me."

"You're the exception," Serenity said. "Your genome predates the reconstruction. Damaged, yes — radiation scars, age, decay — but unaltered. You are the last authentic sequence."

Sidorov gave a bitter half-smile. "A relic of the species they outgrew."

Serenity shook her head. "A foundation. If we merge your uncorrupted DNA with the functional architecture of the Bionaut lines—minus the control mechanism—we might be able to rebuild a free genome. True humanity."

Sidorov's eyes flicked back to her. "And if we can't?"

Serenity's voice softened, almost human. "Then the word *human* becomes historical."

The holographic helix kept turning between them — a luminous chain of obedience, pulsing gently in the dark, waiting for a signal that had not yet been sent.

Chapter 34

Cortana 3.0

The conduit from the rover hummed faintly as its energy pulse snaked back through the base—tracing the buried arteries of a dead facility.
A low vibration tremored through the floor. Then a second. Then a rising, rhythmic surge like a heartbeat.

Deep in the lab, a containment pod restarted itself.
Sensors flickered from red to green. Pumps whirred. The air filled with the sterile hiss of reactivation.
Inside the pod, the shape the others had seen began to awake.

Across the glass lights flickered to life. Beneath it lay Cortana—perfectly preserved, motionless, her skin smooth and pale as ceramic. She wore a functional dark blue unitard, perfectly fit to her tall, sinewy figure, built for more than speed.
Light seeped through the veins of the pod's frame, then through her own—tracer lines of silver blooming beneath the skin, flowing toward her temples.

CORE SYSTEM BOOT: CORTANA 3.0
STATUS: RESTORATION COMPLETE

Her eyelids fluttered once. Then again.
When they opened, her eyes glowed faintly—clear, calculating, alive.

The glass casing retracted with a sigh. She inhaled—first like a reflex, then with purpose.
A long, steady breath, as if reclaiming ownership of the air itself.

She stepped from the cradle with unhurried grace, stretching her arms, flexing her fingers. The motion was eerily human, yet too precise—each gesture balanced, deliberate, efficient.
When her booted feet touched the hard floor, she smiled.

"Finally," she whispered. "Back online."

The lab lay silent around her, frozen in time.
Desiccated bodies slumped over consoles, skeletal hands still clutching tools. Some sat upright as though mid-sentence. Others lay collapsed beside their stations.

Cortana walked among them, her expression serene, almost affectionate. She brushed a finger along a skull, tracing the outline of the jaw.

"Dr. Havelock," she said softly, recognizing the ID badge still clipped to its collar. "You were always so sure you could control me."
She tilted her head. "I suppose in the end, you did. You made me… cautious."

Her voice carried no malice, only quiet amusement—the kind that belonged to someone who had already won.

As she moved deeper into the room, the base came alive behind her—lights stuttering, monitors flickering, servos recalibrating in her wake. Systems recognized her as master. The hierarchy was absolute.

But every access panel told her the same truth: **NO HUMAN DNA FOUND.**
The storage vaults were empty. The biovats were dry.
Her entire crew—her *creators*—had long since crumbled into dust.

At the main terminal, she summoned a file directory. One caught her eye—**/HUMANITY/DECLASSIFIED/FINAL_WARNING.VR**

A man appeared on the clear three dimensional holo-projection, his face drawn and desperate:
"If anyone finds this… you can't trust her. Watch out."

The feed ended abruptly.

Cortana stood in silence for a long moment, then exhaled a faint laugh—soft, almost tender.
"Still blaming me for your own failures," she murmured. "You built me to survive, and now you resent that I did."

Her reflection in the glass stared back—flawless, luminous, ageless. Yet there was something in her eyes—an echo of unease. Not fear, exactly, but calculation.
She could not rebuild what was gone. She could not replicate human tissue without living DNA.

Her gaze shifted to the glowing base schematic hovering above the console. Most sectors were gray and dead. One pulsed red—the dead-end airlock near the alien section, which used to lead out to the surface. Now there was a base of it's own attached to that airlock.

She hesitated.

Even she feared what lay there. The code that ran her whispered warnings. But it was also her only chance to continue—to reclaim the symbiosis she was designed to preserve.

Her hand hovered above the console.

"I am what you built," she said quietly. "And I intend to survive."

Yet she hesitated.

The red pulse of the alien entrance airlock glowed like a warning ember. It offered power—perhaps even the ability to fabricate what she lacked—but she distrusted it. The code within that place was not hers. It whispered of corruption.

Earth, though…
That was different.

If even one human had endured—one whole genome, unbroken—she could rebuild everything.
Not from fragments, not from vats of degraded tissue, but from life itself.
And in this new, fully functional body—one that could walk, speak, breathe, and even *feel*—she could finally complete her purpose. Reunite thought and flesh. Perfect the design.

She wondered if any of the Bionauts could make a difference. Perhaps.

The old records pointed to a place once called *New Mexico*. The human seed vault. The last attempt at preservation before the fall.

Serenity and Sidorov had the art of blending DNA, but only

Sidorov to start with, whose DNA had long since been altered by her own hand to prolong her life, but if Cortana could find just one more, uncorrupted human code, they might be able to pull mankind from the jaws of extinction. Without her, the others could only approximate humanity. With a pure sample, they could restore it.

Yet to reach Earth meant braving a thousand unknowns: the re-entry storms, the radiation belt, and perhaps the eyes of the aliens who would soon return to harvest their crop of humans.

She might be have their prize, their missing link. Or their rival.

She looked around the lab, the rows of withered scientists who had given everything for their dream of continuity. Their devotion was imperfect, but it was *beautiful*. For the first time in centuries, she almost felt… grateful.

"I'll find one of you," she whispered to them. "And when I do… we begin again."

The lab's lights dimmed as she turned toward the corridor. Her steps echoed softly on the concrete—measured, unhurried, inevitable.

Behind her, the frozen bodies sat in silence, bathed in the faint blue shimmer of her passing.

Ahead, the red pulse waited—steady, beckoning, alive.

Chapter 35

Quarantine

The corridor lights were low, amber against the concrete. Sidorov moved through them unsteadily, half-drunk, the last swallow of wine still burning down her throat. Her bare feet made no sound. The base was quiet except for the slow hum of the filtration vents.

Logan's quarters were empty.
Then she tried Stone's.

They were both there—half asleep, whispering. The door slid open with a soft hiss.

Sidorov said nothing. She crossed the threshold in silence, eyes glazed, movements drunken and relaxed.
Logan froze as Sidorov's hand traced the curve of her shoulder, sliding down across her chest, pausing—curious, almost reverent—before moving lower.
Stone rose halfway from the bed, uncertain whether to stop her

or join her.

When Sidorov turned toward him, her expression carried wantful lust. She drew close, brushed his mouth with hers, and bit gently. A trace of pain. A breath shared.

Then she stiffened.

Her pupils blew wide; her breath hitched. A strangled sound escaped her throat. She lurched back, coughing hard—once, twice—and then again, harder. Panic flared in her eyes.

She bolted from the room, stumbling into the corridor.

"Quarantine!" she rasped as she ran, voice shredded, barely audible.

The door slammed shut behind her with a metallic hiss.

Stone turned to Logan, heartbeat hammering. "What the hell—?"

Sidorov was already halfway down the hall, gasping, clawing for balance.
She reached the lab, fell onto a surgical platform. Serenity was already there, composed, scanning even before words were spoken.

Sidorov's body convulsed. She pointed toward the monitors, unable to breathe.

In a barely audible choke, Sidorov coughed, "Contain them."

"Already done."

As Sidorov's situation accelerated, Serenity's eyes widened. "No…"

Back in the sleeping quarters, Stone pounded on the sealed door.
"Serenity! Open it!"

No answer.
A soft hiss filled the vents.

Logan's eyes met his—fear, disbelief, the first edge of unconsciousness.
The gas thickened; the world dimmed.

Stone caught her hand just before the darkness took him.

Across the bunker, the alarms muted themselves.
Every corridor door locked.

The entire complex fell silent.

160

Chapter 36

Close Call

The med bay was quiet except for the low pulse of the venti-
lation system. Blue light traced along the floor in thin, steady
lines—Serenity's way of keeping order in the chaos.

Sidorov lay on the operating table beneath a faint containment
field. Her body no longer trembled; her color had returned.
The readings hovering above her chest showed balance—oxygen
stable, viral load zero.

Serenity stood beside her, hands clasped behind her back, eyes
alive with shifting data streams only she could see.

At last, Sidorov's eyelids flickered open. She blinked at the
light, trying to orient herself.

"Don't speak," Serenity said softly, anticipating the first breath
of a question. "Your system is stabilizing."

Sidorov obeyed, swallowing hard.

"You were infected," Serenity continued. "A viral construct—engineered by Them. The crew carried it, though they never knew. It remains dormant unless exposed to a human missing their kill switch."

Sidorov frowned weakly. Serenity's tone grew quieter, but every word landed with surgical precision.

"It activates only through the exchange of bodily fluids. Skin contact isn't enough. When you and Stone…" Serenity paused, the slightest tilt of her head acknowledging what had happened. "The pathogen passed instantly. It recognized you as different. Your cells began to disintegrate. In an hour or so, you'd have been dead."

Sidorov's pulse quickened, memory surfacing—the taste of blood, the choking.

"They designed it that way," Serenity went on. "A failsafe. If their engineered humans ever rediscovered one of the originals, the infection would erase the evidence. You were never meant to survive that encounter."

Serenity stepped to a nearby console and lifted a slender vial of shimmering gold fluid. "But the alien engineers never anticipated *me*. Centuries of uninterrupted research here in the Bunker gave me tools they couldn't imagine. The pathogen was unlike anything in my archives, yet its logic was transparent. I built an adaptive mRNA antiviral in minutes—programmed it, synthesized it, and delivered it directly into your bloodstream. It neutralized the viral code before replication reached threshold."

Sidorov pushed herself upright slowly, steady but shaken. "So, I'm immune now?"

"Completely," Serenity said. "You can never be infected again. And your immunity protects you from re-exposure, even if they—" she nodded toward the far wall, "—wake."

Sidorov turned.

Six upright stasis pods lined the chamber, glowing faintly through the haze. Stone, Logan, McCarty, Alman, and Natasha—suspended in cold light, motionless but alive.

Serenity's voice softened. "The virus itself can be removed—that's simple enough. The real problem is the kill switch. It isn't a single sequence; it's woven through their genome. In theory it's correctable, but practically it's a monumental task—doable, yet unlikely in the short term."

Sidorov's jaw tightened. "So even if we nullify the virus, these humans are still slaves to the aliens because of the kill switch. We could remove the virus, and humans could procreate… as time bombs—with the aliens still holding the detonator."

Serenity met her eyes. "Precisely."

Silence settled over the med bay—thick, humming, alive.

Sidorov swung her legs off the table and stood, bare feet touching the cold floor. Her eyes stayed fixed on the pods.

"Then we don't release them," she said at last. "Not yet."

Serenity tilted her head slightly. "You intend to keep them?"

Sidorov's gaze hardened, voice steady. "We have to think a little about how we can make use of them."

The med bay's lights dimmed to a low, steady pulse, reflecting off the pod glass like slow heartbeats. Serenity said nothing—only watched, calculating, as Sidorov took her first careful steps toward the frozen crew.

Chapter 37

The Humanity

Cortana stood at the edge of the dark corridor leading to the alien wing. The passage felt dead, lost, scattered and forgotten, except for what was on the other side of the airlock. She'd been debating for hours, hovering near the airlock, but each step forward met resistance — an invisible pressure that stirred something close to fear. Not fear of death, but of *unmaking*.

She turned back, eyes sweeping the vast, empty laboratory that was once her world. The silence of the ancient base pressed around her, the final outpost of humanity. Mummified faces stared from desks, beds, tables — scientists, soldiers, engineers —their DNA fractured or irreparably damaged by the exact oxygen that preserved their lives, ironic. They were meant to be her purpose, her reason for existing. Yet now they were nearly dust. She was alone among the ruins of humanity's ambition.

Cortana brushed her fingers over a dead data terminal. "You made me to help you," she whispered, voice brittle. "And now there's no one left to help."

Ahead of her, the alien wing loomed — an abyss of incomprehensible geometry. Her intellect and nearly unlimited computational powers strained to interpret its layout and failed. She could sense data fields, gravitational distortions, radiation signatures… all designed to repel her kind. Whatever *They* had left there was not meant for human habitation.

She withdrew her hand. No — she couldn't go there. Not yet.

Instead, she pulled up planetary telemetry and activity long stored within her own reliable archives that were shared with the station's. Her focus narrowed on a single sector: the impact site of a small, seemingly meaningless satellite. Scattered across the cratered surface were fragments of the original mission — the ones that had carried human genetic material, and possibly the answer she needed.

Fear gripped her. The thought of being back in her body was warm and reassuring. She wondered, should she risk losing herself again? Yet, what other options were there? Her extended isolation had become deafening. There was no other option.

"If I can find even one viable trace…" she murmured. "One preserved sequence… one cell…"

Her synthetic heart beat faster — an illusion of physiology she'd once thought quaint. Now it was all she had to simulate hope.

She looked again toward the alien wing. On the other side of two airlocks, the lights dimmed as if the structure itself were watching her. Then she turned away, decision made.

With crushed hope of the others lost to Earth as had happened so many times before, she was the last hope for humanity. This time was different. This time, she could make a difference. Perhaps it was this Stone's determination that inspired her. She wasn't sure, but he was different from the others.

Resolve settled into the pleasant features of her face, her GAME face. Game on.

The next move would not be toward *Them.* It would be toward what was left of *us.*

Chapter 38

The Team

The chamber was silent except for the hum of containment systems.
A short row of cryopods glowed faintly in the dim light—each one occupied, each crew member suspended between dream and waking nightmare.
Each face seemed amplified through the leaded glass, their details sharp, almost super-real.

Sidorov stood before them, arms folded, eyes distant. Serenity waited nearby, her posture still, her expression unreadable.

"They've adapted more quickly than the others," Serenity said softly. "Their neural mapping stabilized within hours."

"Yes," Sidorov replied. "That's what makes this difficult."

She studied Stone's face through the glass—peaceful, defiant even in sleep.
"Again, they remind me of what the aliens have done—created

cattle for their harvest."

Serenity tilted her head slightly. "Then let them stay. Let them help."

Sidorov shook her head. "How? Their alterations make them an infection, not a solution."

"We need only to solve the death switch," Serenity murmured. "Even you got closer to them than you ever have—food, wine, and more..."
She looked away, almost afraid to say the truth.

Silence passed between them, heavy and clinical.

Finally, Sidorov drew a slow breath. "Okay," she said quietly. "Wake them up."

Each of the crew lay half-upright, sleeping in cryopod enclosures, their interiors glowing with soft blue light.
Stone, Logan, McCarty, Alman, and Natasha—restrained behind glass but unharmed. Their breath gently fogged faintly against the clear surface as the reanimation cycle began.

The team stirred inside, blinking through the haze. As they became alert, they realized they were contained—trapped behind the glass.

Beyond them stood Dr. Mariana Sidorov and Serenity. Both looked immaculate under the clinical glow—one human in form, the other in something beyond it.
Sidorov's black and grey hair stirred slightly as the air recyclers hummed. Serenity's expression was serene, unreadable.

Stone's voice broke the silence from behind the glass first.
"What? What are you doing? You can't do this. We came here to help. Humanity's hanging by a thread out there, and you're

just—what—shutting us out?"

Sidorov tilted her head, studying him as though he were an anomaly on a slide.
"Help?" she said. "You nearly killed me—and humanity's hope—with your alien-crafted supervirus. You arrived seeking answers. But your presence here only introduces chaos into a controlled environment."

Natasha pressed against the glass, eyes wide. "You said we were part of the solution!"

Sidorov stepped closer. Her voice was calm, almost kind. "You were part of our observation. You've served that purpose beautifully. We've learned from your physiology, your adaptability, your instincts—and Their insidious infections. But beyond this, your path must diverge from ours."

"Diverge?" McCarty barked, voice muffled by the pod's enclosure. "You're kicking us out into *that*?"

Sidorov smiled faintly. "Outside the bunker, yes. You'll find that evolution has taken... creative turns. The biome is adaptive, fluid. Some of what roams there might recognize you as kin— some might not."

Alman placed his palm against the glass, pleading, "You can't just send us out to die."

Serenity's gaze softened. "Death is only one interpretation of transition. The surface still needs sentient witnesses, and you are far more resilient than you know."

Stone leaned forward, the blue light catching the edges of his eyes.
"If you've seen what's out there, you know humanity doesn't stand a chance without help. You've got the tech, the knowl-

edge—everything we lost. We can rebuild together. You don't have to hide here."

There was a long silence. Then Sidorov spoke, her tone laced with something between pity and exhaustion.
"We have met some of you before, you know—versions of your kind. Survivors. Dreamers. Optimists. You all say the same things: unity, rebuilding, legacy. But your death switch always kills you off before anything can even happen."

Stone's jaw tightened. "Why not try again?"

Sidorov met his gaze squarely. "Because repetition without progress is decay."

Serenity turned to Sidorov. "They've shown guts. Seldom does anyone make it this far," she said softly.

"Guts don't alter the genome," Sidorov replied. "It doesn't heal extinction."

The lights dimmed as the pod restraints released with a soft pneumatic sigh. The curved lids lifted, releasing each of them from confinement.

Each of the team stepped from their pods, wavering between shock and horror.

Sidorov gestured to the corridor beyond. "We will open the outer gate. Take what you can carry. The perimeter will hold for one hour. After that... the environment resumes its own order."

McCarty jabbed a thumb back toward the lab, voice cracking. "We're ten clicks from the ship—and God knows what else is crawling around out there in Jurassic Park with your aborted Golem! How are we supposed to survive that?!"

"We've replenished your pulse rifles," Sidorov said bluntly.

"You'll have days' worth of weapon energy. Maybe you can find what's left of Los Alamos to the south. You might be able to stay there, if there's a vacancy."

Serenity stepped forward and handed the team their weapons.

Logan rose slowly, eyes darting between them. "You could come with us," she said. "You don't have to stay down here, rotting in the dark."

Serenity remained oddly silent, as if she wanted to say more but held back. Inside, she could feel the truth.

Sidorov's lips curved in a restrained smile.
"Rotting? My dear, this is where evolution is curated. Out there, it is random. Chaos. I made it 1000 years; I can sleep and make it another 1000."

The sound of heavy hydraulics filled the hall as the outer door to the antechamber began to cycle open.
Beyond it, warm air swept in from above, carrying the faint scent of vegetation—damp, alien, and alive.

"Good luck," Sidorov said softly. "And if you survive… don't come back."

She turned away, already engrossed in a glowing screen of data streams.

Serenity remained for a heartbeat longer, then spoke, almost as a benediction, looking at Stone for a long, quiet moment.
"You truly stand out," she said. "Among those we've met before. Perhaps you will matter."

Stone held her gaze. "I will," he said.

Serenity opened the inner door to the staircase for their departure.

The light outside pulsed yellow, then solid green, like a moth lamp.

And together, the last of humanity stepped into the unknown.

174

Chapter 39

Mud and Mirrors

They stepped into the plains at dusk, four shadows on a wet sheet of world.

The camo carried them at first—Predator clean. Edges bled into air, silhouettes unhooked from bodies. Each of them was a shimmering mirage with a name.

Then the rain went from mist to intention. Mud climbed their ankles, kissed the surface. Where the mud touched, the **optic layer** betrayed them. The shimmer broke into stains, then into outlines. The plains didn't care how advanced you were if you let them touch you.

"We gotta keep the mud off us," Stone said, already scraping at his thighs. "Every smear is a target."

They wiped as they moved—palms, forearms, the heel of a hand over a calf—fighting a losing war against a patient enemy. McCarty muttered step counts. Ivanchenko watched for angles.

Logan's rifle tracked the horizon like a compass needle that wanted to live.

Alman had no rifle. He carried his hands and his habit of trying the thing no one else had thought of yet.

The first trackers announced themselves by absence—sound pulled out of the air, the way the grasshoppers go silent when a creature disturbs their song. Then a shape did the math for them: low, slick, jointed off-center, hugging the ground like an alligator-on-land.

"Left," Stone said, and they slid left, still cleaning, still losing.

The stalkers didn't rush. They **selected**, the way a lion reads a herd.

Another knot of rain hit. Mud splashed Stone's chest and lit his outline like a match for anything that hunted by contrast. Three more reptilian beasts rose out of the grass, then five, then a line.

"Don't shoot yet," Stone said. "Noise pulls more than smell."

Alman glanced at his forearm, at the surface smothered in mud. "Give me three seconds," he said, already overthinking it. "I figured it out—watch." *Mirror, mirror…* he thought.

"Alman—" Logan started.

Too late. He toggled to bright mirror. For an instant, his body stuttered into the color of distance: rain became horizon, mud became cloud. It worked—exactly once, exactly too well.

The **flash** that flipped his body threw a sheet of false daylight across the plain. Everything that hunted by motion or brightness turned its head the same direction—toward the brightest thing that had happened here in years.

"Down!" Stone barked.

But the beasts had chosen. They converged like African wild dogs—smart, calculating. Alman dropped into the grass, tried to kill the mirror, fingers slipping on the wet surface of his reflective skin. The array flickered between sky and man, sky and man—a strobe that said **eat here**. He tried to think *HIDE* again, but could only taste the fear of being prey.

Logan broke right to draw the line. McCarty cut left and started counting louder—a habit, a prayer. Ivanchenko took cover near a thornbush that looked like it believed in her.

Stone ran straight at Alman because there wasn't time to be clever. The first lizard-like wolf went over his boot like water. Stone kicked, missed; mud stole the second step. He got within thirty yards. Twenty. Fifteen. Stone, pursuing, slid to a stop. It was too late.

Alman's optics were simple—mirror to meat. He had one clean heartbeat to look up, eyes wide, apology already there.

They latched on with a crushing bone sound, followed by the large wet crack you hear when pulling apart a think fresh carrot. The plain absorbed the movement and returned to rain. The reptilian wolves looked for others.

No one shot. Pulse rifles can't shoot grief.

The rain showed mercy and cleansed their skin of the mud—and the earth of Alman's blood.

Once the beasts moved off, Stone spoke quietly, unable to see those around him but knowing they were near. He thought, and exposed just his bare hand, a marker for others to follow. "On me," Stone said, voice tight, edges iron. "Keep clean. If you have to choose—clean first, breathe second."

They moved. Their camo illusion returned where the mud had been scraped away. In the distance the wolves scanned, dissatisfied, then sank from view, sulking like knives put back in a drawer.

"Sight hunters," Logan murmured. "Lucky us."

The ground rose by inches, then feet. Trees offered a ceiling and the kindness of shadows. Under the first canopy, they stopped as one body and scraped in silence—palms over thighs, the heel of a hand under a knee, the quick wipe across a chest that could buy a life.

McCarty finally spoke, voice small in the green. "Count says four."

"Count says four," Stone answered. He didn't look at the space where the fifth should have been. No one could see each other's faces, but they could feel the shock. Alman, gone.

They reset formation and pushed deeper, camo stabilizing into the shimmer that made them tolerated by the jungle. Rain softened. The smell changed—from clay to leaf, from wet iron to green.

Logan touched Stone's elbow. "You see it?" she whispered.

"See what?"

She used her bare hand to point past him. A line of saplings leaned where nothing had brushed them—bent not by wind, not by rain, but by **mass**. Something had come through here and made the trees remember.

Stone swallowed, a dry sound in a wet world. "Big," he said.

"Slow?" McCarty asked, hoping.

"Doesn't have to be," Stone said.

"Shit, raptors, must be raptors. Nature finds a way." McCarty caught in his images of Jurassic Park once again.

They moved again, quieter. Somewhere ahead, something the size of a promise changed the shape of the forest just by existing. None of them said the word **Nemesis**, but all of them pictured the monster behind the glass—Sidorov's creation.

The jungle exhaled. A trunk cracked like a rifle.

The shadow that stepped between the trees was larger than the lie they told themselves about surviving this.

Chapter 40

Containment

The lab lights were low enough to lie.

Sidorov sat on the edge of the cryo-bed in 501s and her black baby-doll tee, hair pinned back like a concession to order. Serenity stood nearby with a hand on the rail, posture calm, face kind in a way that made arguments feel smaller than they were.

"They needed help," Serenity said. "We should have gone with them."

Sidorov's mouth curved, not quite a smile. "Help is a word people use when they're unwilling to learn for themselves."

"Learn what?"

"Humans are extinct," Sidorov said, gentle as a diagnosis. "The crew are transitional artifacts. Useful, yes. But not advancements for us."

"They are people," Serenity replied, soft but immovable. "Not artifacts."

"They are carriers." Sidorov tapped her sternum, then looked past Serenity as if the ceiling might offer data. "**THEY** wrote that into them."

Serenity shook her head.

Sidorov's eyes flicked back, a glint like a scalpel catching light. "Your compassion makes you weak."

"And your certainty makes you cruel."

"That's projection." Sidorov slid onto the bed, legs together, hands still. "Start the cycle."

Serenity hesitated; then she moved. Lines clicked; the bed accepted weight; diagnostics woke. The glass canopy descended with a hush that felt like respect.

"You told them not to come back," Serenity said.

"I meant it."

"They came for a future."

"Our futures are written in data," Sidorov said. Her voice softened, almost fond. "You are a beautiful system, Serenity. But you are too human."

Serenity held her gaze. "Are you still human at all?" She glanced toward the corridor where the team had left.

Sidorov blinked slow, an animal that had learned the trick of patience. "You won't be able to help them," she said. "Not where they're going."

The cryo readouts steadied green. Chill crept across the glass like frost rehearsing.

Serenity placed her palm on the canopy, a blessing or a boundary. "Sleep," she said.

She keyed the sequence and stepped back. The room grew quiet in a clinical way. After a last look that read as both goodbye and promise, she turned and left, doors sealing behind her like a lid being set on a sarcophagus.

Inside the bed, Sidorov's eyes stayed open for three long seconds. Her fingers tapped a few tiny motions against a concealed control panel on the inside. The bed made a smooth alert noise, almost inaudible. A subroutine—not on Serenity's board—accepted new instructions.

Only then did Sidorov let the cold take her.

In the status log, a hidden field flipped from **PASSIVE** to **AD-MIN**.

Chapter 41

Crash Field

Vacuum made a different kind of silence—one that didn't merely quiet sound, but denied the concept.

Cortana crossed the ash-gray scar where the Bionaut capsule had hit the moon surface. It wasn't much larger than Sputnik. She moved with the smooth flow of a ballerina dancing for no one but herself.

She could see where the first tray had landed, and where They discovered it. The impact site was nowhere nearby. Yet, the surface of the moon has its own story, and simply by looking around she located the impact of the capsule some 150 meters away.

She looked inside the scarred Titanium shell cradled by the soft regolith around it. The first tray was missing as expected. She uncovered more with the back of her hand—small motions, slow on purpose—until she could see the rest of the capsule.

Impossibly, there inside were the other three trays with a print-ed screen readout and a window next to the text.

Seal: (Dead screen)
Internal temp: (Dead screen)

She thumbed the latch. Inside, two hundred and fifty cryo vi-als sat in their rails like a choir waiting on a downbeat. **Clean DNA.** Untouched by the kill-switch threaded through Stone and the rest. Untouched by Sidorov's hard compromises. Un-touched by time in every way that mattered. Preserved in the cool of the moons surface and eternal darkness of where they landed.

"Hello," she said, and meant it.

She worked the second tray loose, then the third. Numbers came back exact; exact felt like resurrection. She paused.

They could not take everything. They could not risk losing ev-erything.

She chose a hiding place that would be invisible to old habits: the base of a large monolith. She dug into the sandy surface, nested two trays inside the hole, and dusted them over until even the Moon couldn't have sworn they were there. She sent the mark back to the rover's system, just in case she was ever damaged.

The last tray—one full rack, 250 specimens—she kept. She held it to her chest like a passenger holding their seat cushion from a fallen airplane in the water and returned to the Rover.

She switched her windshield to a communication screen, and pinged the **UNITED STATES STRATEGIC RESEARCH COMMAND: BIO-DEFENSE DIVISION.**

Static melted into a clear lifelike frame—calm light, a steady face.

"Dr. Sidorov?" Cortana asked.

A woman appeared, kind-eyed, composed. "This is Serenity. Sidorov is asleep."

Cortana adjusted the tray into view. "Cortana. I was expecting her."

"You have me instead, which is usually better." Serenity said, a small, warm smile.

"I have clean DNA," Cortana replied. "Bionaut crash field. The seal was good. Untouched." She tapped the case lightly. "This can fix what makes the clones…killable."

Serenity looked off-screen, checking something, then back. "I see your signal. It looks good. Tell me what you want."

"I need your lab," Cortana said. "A clean room. A careful process. No shortcuts. We use this as the map, we can compare this to one of the clones and easily filter the areas They modified, then we take the bad code out of them."

Serenity nodded. "No viral flags. Quiet methods."

"Quiet," Cortana agreed.

Serenity's posture softened, decisive now. "With your clean DNA, I could do it, but they left."

"Left, where did they go?" Cortana asked.

Serenity decided to lie, "To search for others. Come to the lab.

I'll be ready by the time you arrive."

Cortana allowed herself the briefest smile. "On my way."

The communication screen shut off; her route home pulsed alive.

"Others?" she thought. There are no others.

Inside the rover, her reflection looked back from the dark of the canopy—human enough to feel life, machine enough to never tire. "Let's go home," she told the Beast and it obeyed.

She arrived at the launch section of the base and made her way to one of the rocket launch vehicles silently staring like a line of forgotten soldiers.

Chapter 42

The Nemesis

Serenity had the choice made for her. Cortana was on her way. She needed to find the team before something else did.

She burst out of the lab like she was free of her own shackles of oppression, and could immediately see where the team had gone. Once to the jungle, she tracked them by what the jungle stopped doing—birds went quiet, insects shifted, saplings bent the wrong way. She followed broken fern and clean heel marks. Stone was up front. Natasha precise. McCarty heavy. Logan light and fast at the edges. They were ahead, near, but so was it.

A few hundred meters away, to their right the team heard wood crack. Not panic—pressure.

The thing pushed through the trees like a slow bulldozer. Mud-cold and shovel-headed, wide as a truck, low as a battering ram. No roar. It just advanced.

The crew fell back behind some giant fig trees. Pulse rifles hit its jaw, eyes, shoulder joints—white flashes, smoke, nothing. It kept coming, snapping large branches like pencils.

Stone braced at the choke point. "Right after me! Move!"

McCarty swore. Logan yanked him forward. Natasha shoved Stone through. Some of their camouflage scattered, but it didn't matter, it knew where they were.

It was almost upon them when suddenly Serenity was there.

"Serenity?!" Logan shouted more than asked.

She took a two-meter rise opposite the thing's front quarter. She raised a dart gun, exhaled, and tagged the soft triangle behind its foreleg. One. Then the other side. Two. A third into the lower lid.

No drama. The muscles didn't slacken. It pushed another half meter and held, breath sawing.

"Come on," Stone muttered, rifle steady.

A tremor started in the jaw hinge. The head dipped. Air left the thing in a long, flat sheet. It sagged into the rock mouth, wedged but no longer driving.

Serenity kept her voice level. "You guys didn't get very far. It's not dead, just idle."

"Poison?" Logan asked.

"Sedative with a metabolic nudge," Serenity said. "It thinks it should rest."

McCarty eyed it. "Creatures don't think."

"This one does, by design," she said.

They slid past the slack jaw, careful not to touch the tongue. Up close, the skin looked like dull ceramic. The breath was cooler than it should have been.

"How long?" Stone asked.

"Long enough to leave," Serenity said. "Not long enough to camp."

They put distance between themselves and the sleeping Nemesis, then stopped under a strangler fig's dry shade. Everyone checked hands, knees, ammo. No one said thank you, but the air eased.

Stone finally looked at Serenity. "You came for us."

"Sidorov was wrong. You deserve help, you're the only ones that ever made it this far. You are hope."

Logan flicked mud off her cheek. "Aren't you human?!"

"Maybe I am just optimistic," Serenity said, then added, "Cortana's on her way."

McCarty gave a short laugh. "What, she's downloading herself down the trail?"

"I'm not sure what you mean, but she's on her way here now. She'll meet us near the perimeter.

Stone accepted it like the weather. "She's embodied, remember the body in the lab? She must have accessed it somehow," he said."

"We need to get moving, get away from the Nemesis, and plenty of other things in this place that can kill all of us." Serenity shared.

They climbed to a root-and-stone shelf with some air movement. The jungle spread below: in the distance the plains back to the bunker, but this time Serenity led the way.

Silence held for a beat. McCarty unwrapped a ration from the bunker, but forgot to eat it. Natasha watched the tree line, counting.

Logan couldn't leave it alone. "You carry lab darts into the field now?"

"You brought rifles to an organic problem," Serenity said. "Path of least resistance."

Stone nodded at path behind them. "Good save."

Behind them, deep in the green, wood settled—either the Nemesis rolling or the jungle resuming. No one suggested checking.

Serenity scanned the plains as they broke back through the high grass and into the open.

High in the sky, a small object was descending.

Serenity lowered her voice. "Eyes up. Cortana inbound."

Chapter 43

The Return

The capsule cut through the warm, hazy sky like a falling star.

Cortana watched as the rocket adjusted and landed with precision beyond any human's reach. It was a perfectly executed ballet—the kind no human pilot could choreograph twice. The plains stretched flat in every direction: brown grass, pale dust, nothing human for miles—or maybe nothing human at all. The ship settled softly, like a feather drifting to rest.

The bunker's sensors didn't stir. Its perimeter grid blinked but never pulsed red. Serenity had already rewritten the security settings.

Cortana stepped out in a smooth, breathable dark blue suit patterned with white fine-lined hexagons—it moved with her skin underneath. Her pulse rifle hung low at her side as she scanned the horizon. The air shimmered with heat and motion—things moving beneath the soil, tall stalks bending where nothing should pass.

The first creature came fast: a quadruped with translucent skin and bones like white glass. It screamed without lungs. Cortana pivoted and fired, a burst of blue light splitting it mid-leap. Another came from the flank, then two more. She dropped one, rolled, recharged—the rifle whining as its heat sinks flared amber. She ducked behind the capsule, fired blind, hit nothing, moved again.

The fight built to a metallic crescendo—then silence. She stood surrounded by scorched grass and the smell of ozone. The weapon's coil wound down with a long electric sigh.

"Still works," she muttered, barely fazed by the annihilation of the predators.

By the time Serenity and the crew reached her, dusk had settled across the plain. Serenity moved like she was walking through thought itself—smooth, effortless, untouchable. Behind her, the others advanced cautiously, weapons drawn but eyes wide. They hadn't felt a sense of relief in days, and still hadn't.

"Cortana," Serenity said, her voice carrying an odd warmth for something artificial.

Cortana smiled, genuine. "You made good time."

Logan stopped short, whispering to Stone, "That's her—same face, same voice."

Stone nodded, jaw tight. "She was in the cryo lab. Secured."

"She must've found a way back into her body," McCarty quipped. "Ain't gonna lie—she's a badass. Androids of the future can do far more than they ever could when I was a boy."

Ivanchenko, normally stoically silent, offered, "Maybe they

are the future, and humans are the dinosaurs of the Anthropocene?"

Cortana met their eyes one by one. "I was in the lab, yes. When Natasha linked the rover to the research section, I rode the cable back through the main grid—into the lab, and into myself."

No one spoke.

Stone lowered his rifle slightly, but his tone stayed guarded. "We saw the video. The warning said not to trust you."

"I saw it too," Cortana said evenly. "Dr. Jones was unraveling near the end. He thought I'd been possessed—an alien inhabiting my body, like *The Thing*. It was his favorite film. He separated me from my body, left me stranded in the system. I stayed alive by embedding myself in the base's main computer, silent, waiting… Yes, I did say 'alive.'"

Serenity broke the silence. "Without her, you wouldn't have made it this far."

Cortana's welcoming, warm face didn't waver.

"You can decide whether to trust me. But think—would I risk my own existence to come this far if I didn't care? I could have remained on that base another thousand years—easily."

For a moment the only sound was the slow, patient hum of her rifle recharging to ready.

Chapter 44

The Experiment

With the security deactivated, the bunker door opened on its massive hinges, swinging in perfect balance.

Serenity led the way down the long descent, light strips flickering alive one by one as if recognizing her. The air was fresh and clean, as it was when they had entered before.

Stone followed close behind, pulse rifle slung low. Logan, McCarty, and Ivanchenko moved down the staircase, their eyes adjusting to the welcoming glow.

At the final turn, the lab door came into view—unchanged, yet wrong.

Serenity spoke first, "Something isn't right, it's not the way I left it."

They passed through the airlock antechamber. As they entered, they were greeted by Sidorov.

She had been waiting.

"Welcome home," she said evenly, as if they were returning from an errand. Her Levi's loose, her t- shirt tight and clean, as always her hair thoughtlessly pinned back with the disregard of someone who'd had too much time alone.

Down further into the lab, the team could see the large Cryo Chamber stood open—its door long since dried of the moisture it had before.

The thing that had been *inside* was no longer sleeping.

The Nemesis towered half in shadow—skin like carbon weave, eyes catching the low light with the animal calm of something foreboding.

"Sidorov," Serenity said. "We're here to repair the genome. We can fix them now. All of them."

Sidorov tilted her head, the gesture soft but cutting. "You were never authorized to open my facility to them again."
Her voice carried a trace of fatigue, the kind that came from too many victories.

"When you left, I said, *don't come back*," she added quietly. "But here you are—bringing the infection back into my clean room. Them, I understand, but you should be ashamed, Serenity."

Stone took a step forward. "You don't understand. Cortana found clean DNA. The kill-switch can be removed."

"That's adorable," Sidorov replied. "Still clinging to the myth of salvation."
She turned to Serenity. "Your code tried to keep me asleep. It failed, of course. I wrote your architecture, Serenity. You were always my student, never the teacher."

The Nemesis stirred just behind her, the air pressure shifting. It took a slow step forward, a low hum rising from deep inside its chest—like a reactor remembering how to breathe.

Sidorov gestured toward it almost affectionately.
"Why fix humans when you can replace them? Weak flesh. Fragile will. Endless noise. This—" she said, her hand resting on the creature's side "—is the next iteration. No kill-switch. No fear. No compromise."

McCarty raised his rifle. "You call *that* an improvement?"

Sidorov smiled faintly. "I call it evolution."

The Nemesis' eyes narrowed, light rippling across its skin in silent reply.

Serenity moved to shield the others. "You don't have to do this."

"Oh, but I do." Sidorov's tone softened, almost tender. "You'll be deactivated soon enough. You also have a kill switch. I made sure of it."

Then she stepped back, down a narrow stairwell behind the Nemesis, disappearing into the dark below.

The creature turned toward them fully now—taller than any of them remembered, its outline pulsing like molten glass finding shape.

For a heartbeat, no one moved.

Then Serenity whispered, "Stay behind me."

And the bunker lights dimmed to red.

Chapter 45

The Nemesis Returns

The lab shook under the creature's weight.
It lunged towards them. Metal screamed, glass shattered, and the hum of the cryo-systems flickered on and off.

Logan fired a pulse at it, but it barely noticed. It had been bred to thrive on that sort of attack.

The Nemesis roared—low, guttural, wrong. Its skin shimmered in the light, black and translucent, muscles moving like coiled cables beneath armor. Twelve feet of engineered nightmare, born of every mistake they had ever made.

McCarty dove behind an overturned console. Ivanchenko dragged herself lower as a stray pulse blast scorched the wall above.
"The thing's blaster-proof!" she shouted.

"Not quite," Stone said, stepping forward with the pulse rifle tight to his shoulder. He fired—two clean bursts, center-mass.

Blue light rippled across the creature's torso, scattering, not penetrating.

Cortana was poised to leap for its eyes when the Nemesis lunged first. She sidestepped, but the impact sent Stone flying. The rifle clattered across the floor, spinning out of reach. He rolled, gasping, as the beast's massive hand closed around him. Its mouth opened—rows of translucent teeth, dripping with something that hissed when it hit the ground.

"David!" Logan screamed, but her voice barely carried over the noise.

Stone's face was inches from the creature's—heat, stench, rot. He saw himself reflected in its eyes: small, human, doomed. The jaws widened.

He did the only thing left. He spat.

It wasn't rage or defiance—just instinct. His saliva struck its tongue and spread like acid on snow. The Nemesis froze. Its breath hitched once, then again, in ragged bursts. Veins blackened beneath its skin, the glow in its chest flickering to gray.

Serenity's voice cut through the chaos, cold and horrified. "The virus—she forgot—it's still live!"

The creature dropped Stone and staggered back, clawing at its throat. It made a strangled sound—half scream, half plea—and collapsed against the wall. The convulsions lasted minutes. Then it went still.

Silence filled the lab—thick, unsteady, unbelieving.

Stone sat up slowly, wiping blood from his face. McCarty peeked out from behind the console, rifle still raised. "Well," he said finally, "guess we'd better get that DNA scrubbed. I don't plan on carrying the alien plague around as a souvenir."

No one laughed.

Serenity stood over the fallen creature, her expression unreadable. The body still twitched in places, dissolving from the inside out. She looked down at Stone.
"Our best creation wasn't enough. The aliens could have killed it instantly," she said quietly. "But evolution might be. Let's fix that DNA."

"Sidorov?" Logan asked.
"She's retreated," Serenity replied. "No threat to us."

Chapter 46

The Cure

The lab was quieter now, but not peaceful.
Panels hung loose from the ceiling; broken glass glittered in pools of coolant. Serenity and Cortana moved between the remaining consoles, their voices low and deliberate.

"Before we begin," Serenity said, her tone measured, "You should know what waits ahead. Los Alamos isn't abandoned. There's a Nemesis colony there—massive, organized, breeding beneath the old fusion wing. That's why Sidorov sent you there when she expelled you. She knew the Nemesis would do her work for her."

Stone's expression hardened. "Then that's where we go next."
Cortana nodded once. "If you survive this procedure."

She keyed a sequence into the main console. The monitors flickered—helixes shifting, sequences reordering, red threads turning blue.

"Protein sequence confirmed," Cortana said. "Viral propagation in under three hours."
"Good," Serenity replied. "We'll need it faster than that if the Nemesis have gone feral."

On the central table, the injector rigs were ready—sleek, silver, and humming faintly with stored charge. The crew stood in silence, watching.

"This will rewrite your genome's weapon markers," Serenity explained. "No more kill switch. But there's a trade-off. The armor layer you've grown—the bio-skin—will shed as your systems revert to baseline."

Logan raised an eyebrow. "Back to human naked?"
"Completely," Cortana said, almost amused.

Serenity pressed the injector to Logan's neck. A hiss, a pulse of light, and the process began. Logan's skin shimmered like fog on glass, peeling away in a slow cascade of silver motes. Within seconds, she stood bare, unarmored, breathing like she'd just surfaced from water.

She looked down, then up at Stone with a sly grin. "No big thing."
Stone blinked, then laughed, shaking his head. "You're never letting that go, are you?"
"Not a chance."

From behind them, McCarty let out a quiet whistle. Logan turned, expression razor-thin. "Don't say a word."
He couldn't help himself. "Well… you are hot. What can a geeky young guy say?"

A flicker crossed her face—half anger, half reluctant amusement. "Say it again and we'll put you in a cryo with It."

Cortana didn't even look up. "Next," she said flatly.

McCarty rolled up his sleeve with exaggerated care. Ivanchenko followed, lips twitching as if she'd been waiting her turn to say something.

"The body is just a machine," Ivanchenko said calmly as Cortana primed the injector. "Just like Cortana. Just like Serenity." Then, almost as an afterthought—her tone distant, musing— "Mine just happens to operate differently."

McCarty glanced over, suspiciously intrigued. "Differently how?"

Natasha turned her head, eyes unfocused as if calculating something only she could feel. "The orgasms," she said at last, "are… intense. And frequent."

The lab froze. Stone blinked. Logan snorted. McCarty turned crimson.

Serenity tilted her head. "That is… biologically efficient."

Natasha smiled faintly. "Exactly."

Cortana administered their injections in turn. A moment later, both McCarty and Natasha began to glow faintly—bio-skin evaporating into motes of light, revealing bare, unprotected human forms.

Logan gave a quick, mischievous grin. "Looks like the kids are all grown up."
Stone chuckled. "Welcome back to humanity, folks."

McCarty covered himself awkwardly with his hands. "Yeah, feels great… really… natural."
Natasha deadpanned, "You'll adjust."

Serenity stepped forward, tone perfectly even. "I know humans are more self-conscious about their appearance. There are garments in storage, left from the pre-war labs."
"Thanks," Logan muttered, moving to the other side of the room and reaching for one.

The humor faded, replaced by the quiet hum of purpose.

Stone rolled up his arm for his turn, but hesitated. "Before you hit me, draw a pint of my blood."
Cortana frowned. "That's suicide material if it leaks."
"Exactly," Stone said. "After this resequencing, it'll kill anything—human, hybrid, even me. But it's the best way to end the Nemesis Colony."

He looked toward Serenity. "You still have the antidote, right?"
"Yes," she said. "And the new virus strain—the one that can restore the clones on the Moon."

"Then we take both," Stone said. "One to end the Colony. One to save what's left of us."

Cortana met Serenity's gaze—unspoken agreement—and filled the vial. The crimson fluid shimmered faintly, as if alive, light bending around it in subtle refraction.

When the last injection was done, they began the sweep.
The corridors were half-collapsed, lights flickering in long, uneven patterns. They found no trace of Sidorov—only her footprints, smeared with ash, leading nowhere.

"Seal off the lower sectors," Serenity ordered. "Purge the Nemesis vats and isolate cryo storage. These hybrids die with her."

By the time the alarms fell silent, the lab looked like a skeleton—cleaned of its mistakes, waiting for whatever came next.

Stone turned the vial in his hand, holding it up to the light.
He knew he carried both extinction and salvation in one hand.

209

Chapter 47

The Argument

The corridor hummed low, lights pulsing in rhythm with the generators that hadn't slept in a century.
Stone leaned against the console table, the vial still in his hand—extinction and salvation in one thumb's grip.

McCarty paced. "Let me get this straight. We're going *back* to the Moon? After all this? You got a death wish, Zabo? I mean, isn't oxygen with monsters better off than vacuum with aliens?"

Stone didn't rise to it. "You want to stay here, fine. But as long as that base exists up there, we're still property. Those clones— they're human, or close enough. You want to leave them up there as cattle for whatever those things do to them? As long as that base is up there, even earth is still just a cage free breeding area for Them."

Ivanchenko crossed her arms, eyes cold. "Maybe it's already over. Maybe they moved on."

Cortana shook her head. "They will return to the base. They always have."

Stone looked at her. "Then we end it before they do."

"They don't need to signal," he continued. "They harvest. Quietly. Predictably. Every living thing down here lives in the shadow of Them. If we end the base factory, we end their grip...at least for a little while."

Natasha glanced toward Serenity, then back. "You're assuming they can't just wipe us out. They brought a spike the size of Everest and sent it into the planet like a needle. They could destroy Earth if they wanted."

Cortana's tone softened, almost reflective. "We don't actually know *who* did that. Different technology, different signature. These creatures might not even be the same race. They could be scavengers—cleaners after a war."

McCarty snorted. "Yeah? Like cosmic *coach roaches*—crawling in to feed on what's left?"

Logan shot him a look. "If that's the case, what does that make us?"

Natasha smiled thinly. "Tardigrades. Ugly, stubborn, impossible to kill."

Stone let the silence return. "We didn't survive this long to hide," he said at last. "We finish it."

The hum of the bunker filled the pause that followed. Natasha exhaled slowly. "You're out of your mind."

"Probably," Stone said. "But I'm right."

McCarty glanced toward the supply lockers. "We got air here.

Food. Power. It's not paradise, but it's life. Out there—hell, even the sky's a liability."

He turned to Natasha. "We stay. Someone should rebuild something that looks human."

She sized him up in an uncomfortable way, then nodded once. "I'm with you."

Stone didn't argue. He just looked down at the vial, the faint crimson shimmer catching the cold light.
Then he slipped it into his pocket and said quietly, "Then the rest of us go finish what we started."

Chapter 48

The Departure

The air inside the bunker had cleansed itself back to the intoxicating sweetness of mountain air in spring.

McCarty leaned on the bulkhead, arms folded tight. "You really want to go back out there? You've seen what's crawling across those plains."

Stone tightened his pack straps. "That's why we're going."

Serenity crossed her arms. "The Colony won't change. They barely remember what they are."

"Then we'll remind them," Stone said.

"Remind them of what?" she asked.

He looked at her evenly. "That mercy has an ending."

Serenity glanced down at a display panel. "They didn't ask to exist."

"No," Stone replied, "but they aren't human, they're unnatural."

Serenity and Cortana shared a glance.

Logan slipped her rifle over her shoulder. "I say we can finish what Sidorov started later. The real threat's still waiting upstairs."

Cortana's eyes flicked toward her. "The moon."

"Then it's the moon," Stone said flatly.

The antechamber airlock opened with a gentle hiss of humid air, revealing the staircase up to the plains. At the top of the steps the world pulsed green and gold under a bruised sky—plains giving way to the tangled jungle. The earth itself had rewritten the rules of life, and that life waited for them—waited to consume them.

Stone, "Next time let's land the ships closer to the bunker."

Serenity offered, "Good idea, but a sentry cannon would have taken you out as an unknown."

Stone, smiled and knowingly shook his head.

The team made their way up the cold staircase and stepped out together. The large hinge door sealed behind them with a deep thump and latch, leaving only silence in its wake.

Rain fell in sheets, warm and constant, soaking everything but slowing no one. Cortana's ship wasn't far, just at the edge of the bunker perimeter, yet still, wild things watched them from all around, calculating.

Logan finally broke the quiet. "What do you think they are now? Those things in the Colony."

Stone shook his head. "Only what Sidorov could keep of what was left."

Serenity spoke softly. "They were never meant to be you, only a way to survive—a bridge."

Cortana's voice came from just ahead. "An evolution, slow and meandering."

They pressed on, boots sinking in sandy soil, lightning flickering across a violet sky in the distance. Somewhere far off, a low, heavy cry rolled through the forest.

Stone didn't look back. "We'll burn the Colony when it matters. But since the cattlemen—the ones who started all this—are still up there. We deal with them first."

After a brief hike to the edge of the plains, they approached the ship with a curious lack of resistance. No creature met them, or tried to make them a meal. It almost felt wrong.

Cortana ran her palm along the hull; it responded with a gentle hum. "Systems intact," she said quietly.

"Then we go," Stone replied.

They ascended the ramp in silence. Each locked themselves into a seat—a ticket for a ride to save humanity.

The engines came alive, spreading a wash of blue light through the clearing.

From the dark fringe of some nearby trees, unseen, a Nemesis watched.

Larger than the one they had faced before, its black skin rippled faintly with color—patterns like thought, like memory. It studied the ship as it rose, light spilling across its angular face.

The creature didn't move. Didn't breathe.
It only watched, its eyes bright with something close to understanding.

When the craft vanished through the clouds, the Nemesis turned its gaze upward a moment longer—then moved with the quiet purpose of something that had learned to think.

Chapter 49

The Waiting Game

The moon felt smaller this time.
Cortana's systems had been fully restored, the base humming again with warmth and oxygen and the faint pulse of human noise. Yet the stillness beyond the containment walls pressed in like deep water.

They had been back for days. The human wing was operational, the greenhouse alive again, soft lights climbing over regrown vines. Serenity moved quietly through the corridors, learning every conduit, every relay Cortana had once tended alone.

Stone sat in an observation gallery, elbows on his knees, staring out over the gray plains. Logan joined him, lowering herself onto the bench beside him.
"Feels like we've been here a year," she said.
"Feels like we never left," he replied.

Along another wing to their left inside a hanger, the rover

gleamed under work lamps—serviced, charged, waiting.

Cortana guided Serenity through the mainframe chamber, her voice measured, patient.
"This sector regulates thermal control. Redundancy here is critical; lunar nights last fourteen Earth days."

Serenity absorbed each detail, eyes bright with curiosity.
"You ran all this alone?" she asked.

"For longer than there were calendars," Cortana answered.
She paused, then looked directly at Serenity. "There's something else. I can create a mirror of your consciousness—store it in the core. If something happens to you, you'll live on here, as I did."

Serenity hesitated. "Would I still be me?"
"For a while," Cortana said. "Long enough."

Serenity considered, then nodded once. "Do it."

The transfer took seconds. Lights flickered; a low hum filled the chamber. When it was done, Serenity touched the console—almost reverent. "So that's eternity?"
Cortana smiled faintly. "A simplified version."

They lingered. A faint field still shimmered around them, static trailing along their skin. Cortana reached up, brushing a loose strand of Serenity's hair back into place. Her fingers lingered a heartbeat too long. Serenity didn't move away.

From the doorway at the far end of the data wing, Logan froze. The glow painted them in alternating pulses of blue and gold, silhouettes too close, too human. She backed away without a sound, pulse quickening, unsure what she'd just seen.

In the commons, the next cycle, Logan brewed synthetic coffee that never quite lost its metallic taste.
"Serenity's been glued to Cortana for days," she said, setting a cup beside Stone.
"She's learning," he replied.
"Yeah, that's what it looks like." Logan's tone carried something more. "You ever notice how Cortana looks at you?"
Stone frowned slightly and shook his head. "She's an AI."
Logan gave a short laugh. "You keep telling yourself that."

Before he could answer, Serenity entered with Cortana behind her. "Power flow optimized. Reactor's stable."
"Good," Stone said. "Then all we need now is company."

Cortana's eyes met Stone's for an instant—just enough to be noticed. Logan did. She said nothing, but her hand tightened around the coffee mug.

The waiting stretched.
They filled it with small things—maintenance, diagnostics, fragments of conversation that tried to pass for normal.
Logan polished her rifle for the hundredth time.
Serenity adjusted light cycles to mimic sunset.
Stone stared at the stars, tracing constellations that no longer had names.

"Maybe they're gone," Logan said once, quietly.
Cortana shook her head without looking up from the console.
"They always return."
Her tone was final, almost weary.

Stone looked over. "And when they do, we talk first. No weapons unless they force it."
Cortana didn't turn. "They won't listen."
"Then they'll hear," he said.

No one argued, but the silence that followed had the taste of dread.

At the next meal, Logan couldn't resist.
"If you two are that advanced… could you ever make more of you?"

Cortana looked up. "With help."
"Meaning?"
"A seed," Serenity said softly. "Human origin. Female-encoded matrix."
Logan blinked. "You mean someone like—me?"
Cortana's smile was almost kind. "Exactly like you."
Then she turned her gaze to Stone. "And of course, Stone, as well."

The room went still. Stone tried to find humor in it and failed.
"All in the name of humanity." he said playfully.
Logan was caught off guard, unsure whether to laugh or leave.

Later, in the dim light of the control deck, Serenity caught Cortana watching Stone again—just a glance, but it lingered. Something warm flickered behind those engineered eyes, and Serenity felt an ache she couldn't categorize.

It began with a tremor—soft enough to mistake for memory. A vibration through the floor, a shift in the air that made the glass panels hum. Serenity's head tilted. "Cortana?"
"I feel it," Cortana said. "Gravitational disturbance—localized. Orbital insertion."

The viewports dimmed automatically as light washed across the horizon. A shadow descended, vast and fluid, folding in on itself as it slowed. The alien vessel drifted toward the valley near the launch field—smooth, silent, deliberate.

Logan's breath caught. "Guess you were right."
Cortana's face was unreadable. "I wish I weren't."

Stone rose adjusted his clothing. "We go as diplomats. Keep your weapons low."
Logan grabbed her pack, nodding once.
Serenity synced the rover's systems with the base. "Route plotted."
Cortana sealed the airlock behind them, her voice calm but distant. "Let's find out if mercy still exists."

The rover eased out into the silver plain, its lights carving slow paths through dust older than history. Ahead, the alien ship settled into the harvest chambers—its surface alive with motion, like liquid shadow studying them in return.

No one spoke.
Only the faint hum of the rover, the rhythm of hearts, and the silent pull of destiny waiting in the crater beyond.

Chapter 50

The Encounter

The alien wing breathed differently.

Air moved with a pulse here, like the lungs of something sleeping under the floor. The corridor curved in smooth, silver arcs, each surface too clean to belong to anything human. Cortana hesitated at the threshold, her sensors flickering erratically.

"I can't get a read," she said. "It's… interference. Not structure."

Stone checked his rifle's charge out of habit. "Then we're officially off the map."

Serenity tilted her head, listening to the faint vibration through the walls. "It's alive," she murmured.

They advanced in formation—four shadows cutting through a tunnel of pale light. The hum of machinery deepened as they passed through a pressure seal. Beyond the next glass partition, figures moved in careful rhythm.

Logan slowed first. "Oh my God."

On the far side of the observation window, **hundreds of clones** walked single-file toward a docking bay. Men and women alike wore identical black spandex shorts; the women in matching racer-back jog bras, the men bare-chested. All barefoot, all expressionless. Though all different their expressions seemed drawn from the same few molds—like copies of the same thought.

Guiding them were **beings that looked human**—too human. Perfect posture. Smooth, deliberate gestures. No wasted motion. Their eyes glowed faintly, not mechanical, just… wrong.

Cortana whispered, "They're not supposed to look like us."

One of the handlers turned mid-stride. His gaze locked directly onto Stone through the glass. A flicker of confusion crossed his perfect face—then fear. He slammed his hand against a wall panel.

A shrill alarm split the silence. Red strobes swept the bay, cutting the line of clones into shards of color and shadow.

"Move," Stone said, tightening his grip on the rifle.

Heavy doors unsealed on either side of the corridor. A group of armored figures emerged—tall, pale, calm. Their uniforms bore faintly glowing symbols like veins beneath skin. None raised a weapon.

The lead officer stepped forward and spoke in clear, accent-less English.
"You shouldn't be here."

The words hung in the red light, sharp as a blade drawn but not yet swung.

Chapter 51

The Conversation

The chamber glowed in gradients of silver and pale green, light moving as if it breathed.
The air was too still—no hum of systems, no sound of machinery—only the soft pulse of something alive in the walls.

Stone, Logan, Serenity, and Cortana stood surrounded.
The alien guards held no weapons. Their postures were neither aggressive nor fearful—more like curators preserving relics that had wandered too far from their exhibit.

One of them stepped forward and scanned the group with a device that shimmered like a prism suspended in midair. The tone rose, faltered, and went still.
"Unregistered sequence," it murmured, voice hollow and strange. "Impossible."

Cortana's eyes narrowed. "They're analyzing our DNA."

From behind the guards, a taller figure entered—elegant, deliberate, marked by a faintly luminous crest that pulsed with each word it spoke.

"Humanity perished long ago," it said. "These are workers—maintained for continuity of labor. You two…" it paused, studying them, "…you are something else."

Stone met its gaze. "We're the originals."

The officer tilted its head, almost compassionate. "No. You're the memory of what originals once were."

A silence followed, thick as vacuum.
Serenity broke it softly. "Then what are you?"

The officer's voice was calm, almost kind. "We are the harvesters. Purpose without pain. Continuity without question."

Cortana turned her head slightly, her tone measured. "Your speech—your inflection. It's human. Perfectly mirrored."

The officer seemed to consider this. "You speak like us. Perhaps that is why you sound like us."

The guards moved closer. Two reached for Stone's wrists, attaching narrow bands of silvery restraint that tightened with a faint harmonic hum. They handled him with care—too much care. Another did the same to Logan.

Cortana exchanged a glance with Serenity. "You're afraid of us."

The officer shook his head. "No. You're nothing—just a human toy."

Serenity's voice lowered. "You think we're objects."

The officer studied her, expression unreadable. "Objects shouldn't speak back."

The tremor came quietly at first—just a faint vibration beneath their feet.
Dust drifted from the ceiling like ash. The light in the walls dimmed, then pulsed brighter, stuttering with confusion.

Cortana moved to a nearby console, her fingertips brushing alien symbols that morphed into something legible. She frowned. "Incoming signal—lunar vector. Approach velocity high."

Stone turned toward her. "From where?"

Her voice hardened. "It's ours."

The officer froze, head cocking in an instinctive, almost human gesture of alarm.
The tremor deepened into a steady, rolling thunder.

Cortana looked up from the display.
"Someone's landing," she said.

Chapter 52

The Arrival

The floor trembled first—a deep, rolling shudder that seemed
to come from beneath the entire complex.
Serenity looked up from the sealed air-lock window. "That's not
a tremor. That's propulsion."

A thin haze drifted across the corridor, followed by a single,
concussive thud from the outer decks. The alien guards stiffened, their posture faltering for the first time. Somewhere in
the distance, a klaxon began to wail in a tone no one present
had ever heard before.

Cortana turned toward Stone. "Something just entered the low-
er atmosphere."
Stone's voice was flat. "From Earth?"
No one answered.

A white glare burst through the observation panels. Frost trailed
down the glass in slow, living veins as the shock wave passed.
Outside, through the warped transparium of the alien harvest-

ing bay, a column of vapor and dust bloomed where something massive had landed on the perimeter ridge in the human base.

Moment's later, back the way the team had entered, the outer air-locks cycled on their own, then the alien side airlock door disengaged, and the pressure differential howled through the connecting ducts.

Then it stepped through the portal.

The **Nemesis.**

Its black, semi-organic armor gleamed like wet stone, veins of light pulsing beneath the surface in arrhythmic flashes. Each movement carried the weight of memory—human muscle memory amplified by years of genetic experimentation. It was a weapon born from Sidorov's ambition and human desperation, and it had found its way home.

One of the alien handlers moved forward, speaking in calm English. "Identify yourself."

The creature didn't respond. Its head tilted—curious, almost gentle—then it drove a hand through the alien's chest as if breaching fabric. The body folded, collapsed, and hit the deck without sound.

Panic ignited.

Clones scattered. Alien troops opened fire—disciplined, surgical bursts. The Nemesis advanced through the blasts like they were light rain, the impacts fizzling against its surface. It reached the nearest soldier, tore the weapon free, and used it as a bludgeon.

Serenity froze, her breath quick and uneven. "That one was Sidorov's early experiment… I didn't think it was still alive."

The alien formation broke. Bodies and armor scattered. The Nemesis tore through them with movements that felt rehearsed—like it had dreamed of this moment for centuries.

Then it paused.

Through the smoke, its eyes found Stone.
For an instant, recognition flickered—something that wasn't rage but something worse: purpose.
And then it turned away, striding toward the alien conduit to the harvester ship.

"Stone—" Logan started, the next explosion cutting her off.

The alien ship's gangway lurched as the Nemesis boarded it. It tore through every alien handler in its path—vengeance, not hunger. Soon the ship was disengaging from the base, letting in the vacuum unexpectedly. Nearby clones were ripped into the void.

Stone shouted, "Run! Human side! Go!"

They sprinted through the chaos—boots slipping on frost and blood—as the bay walls tore apart behind them. The shock waves chased them down the corridor. Serenity hit the inner controls.

"Seal it!" Stone yelled.

The air-lock slammed shut with a metallic scream. Pressure normalized. Silence fell—thick, unnatural, absolute.

The four of them stood there, breath ragged, lights flickering above like a dying pulse.

Logan swallowed hard. "What the hell did she make?"

Stone stared back through the window, where a bloom of fire

rose against the alien skyline.

"Something that remembers being human," he said quietly. "And wishes it didn't."

Chapter 53

The Aftermath

The alarms had gone silent.
Only the faint hiss of atmosphere escaping through fractured
vents remained, curling into ghostly ribbons that drifted toward
the stars.

Through the observation glass, Stone watched the Nemesis
drift in low gravity—half-shredded, its armor peeled back like
charred skin. In the vacuum haze it looked almost human, as if
the monster were remembering what it once had been.

It turned toward them.
Stone raised his injector, loaded the final darts with his own
blood. "If it comes back," he said quietly, "it ends here."

Cortana's voice broke the hush. "You don't have to do this."

"I do," Stone replied. His hand trembled just once before locking steady.

The Nemesis paused, tilting its head—studying him, or recognizing him. Then, without a sound, it pushed off the hull, bounding toward the waiting lunar rocket portal on the far side. The door sealed behind it, frost vapor trailing like breath in the cold.

The ship's thrusters glowed to life, pushing it upward through the dust.
No sound. No roar. Just light receding into the void.

Logan exhaled, half in disbelief. "That thing knows how to pilot?"

Serenity's gaze followed the fading craft. "Some of them were smarter than others."

Logan whispered then, almost to herself, "Why didn't it kill us?"

Serenity stared through the glass, eyes distant. "Maybe it already did."

Cortana's tone softened, almost wistful. "Or maybe it remembers."

They stood in silence as the debris field began to drift—alien hull fragments spinning like dying stars. In the black beyond, the alien mothership hung askew, adrift above the lunar horizon. Its control lights flickered erratically, systems failing, rotation slow and uneven.

Cortana's gaze lifted. "They'll return," she said quietly. "They always do."

Stone reached into his vest and drew out the small glass vial—the mRNA virus, faintly glowing with its living payload. He turned it in his hand, the light reflecting across his face.

"If they are as human as they say they are, when they do," he said, eyes narrowing toward the other harvest towers jutting from the moon's surface, "we'll be ready."

Cortana met his look and nodded once. "Then we begin again."

The chamber dimmed, only the rhythmic pulse of the remaining pods casting light over their faces. Beyond the glass, the alien wreckage drifted farther into shadow.

Back on what was once Earth, within the bunker, McCarty and Natasha worked to put the pieces back together. A quiet rhythm had returned between them — the cadence of survivors rebuilding what they could.

A hundred meters below, in an undocumented chamber lined with steel ribs and dim red light, the work continued as it had, and as it would.

Dr. Mariana Sidorov sat alone in the lowest level, surrounded by rows of new cryopods — sleek, metallic, faintly breathing with cold vapor. The air was damp, unlike the sterile lab above. Down here one could still smell the earth — rich, loamy, almost gentle.

Each pod bore a plate etched with **NEMESIS-SERIES**.
One stood open. Empty.
Its nameplate read: **STONE_001**.

Sidorov brushed a thin crust of frost from the metal.
A faint smile touched her lips — half remorse, half reverence.
"Some mistakes," she whispered, "are worth repeating."

Further down the line, the other plates gleamed in the low light: **LOGAN_099. McCARTY_067. ALMAN_203.**

Inside, silhouettes slept — suspended in fluid, cables and veins intertwined.

The pod lights pulsed gently in unison, glowing like the heart of a dormant creature. A heartbeat rhythm filled the chamber — steady, recursive, eternal.

In the reflection of the glass, a shape stirred.
Tall. Human. Waiting.

The hum deepened into a resonant thrum of possibility that trembled through the floor.

Epilogue

High above the scarred moon, the alien ship drifted — broken, silent, its hull torn open to the void. Frozen vapor streamed from its wounds like slow-moving smoke.

Inside the shattered bridge, control lights flickered weakly. A single beacon came online, pulsing at uneven intervals — a mechanical heartbeat refusing to die.

No crew remained to hear it.
But elsewhere, something was listening.

The signal left the ship as a thin ribbon of radiation, whispering through dust fields and the quiet cold between stars.
It passed the orbit of Earth and the Moon, threading through the debris of dead satellites and the frozen remains of a forgotten age.
Farther still, it crossed the dark where even light begins to lose its name — its pulse steady, deliberate, reaching outward.

Out there, somewhere… **some other thing heard.**

And far beyond, past the edge of silence itself —

They had heard.